I0737202

LURED BY MAGIC

LOST BY MAGIC: BOOK 3

DAVID NETH

DN Publishing

Lured by Magic
Lost by Magic, Book 3
Copyright © 2023 by David Neth
Batavia, NY

www.DavidNethBooks.com

ISBN: 978-1-945336-47-8
First Edition

Subscribe to the author's newsletter for updates and exclusive content:
DavidNethBooks.com/Newsletter

Follow the author at:
www.facebook.com/DavidNethBooks

Also by David Neth

Lost by Magic
Lost by Magic
Lucky by Magic
Lured by Magic

Coven
Harpy
Siren
Valkyrie
Shapeshifter
Sorcerer
Witch (Short Story)
Enchantress
Oracle
Trickster
Poltergeist
Hex (Short Story)
Witch Hunter
Demon (Short Story)

Under the Moon
The Full Moon
The Harvest Moon
The Blood Moon
The Crescent Moon
The Blue Moon

The Art of Magic

Fuse
Origin
Omertá
Oblivion

Heat
Black Magnet
Dust Storm
The Gatekeeper

Standalone
All I Ever Wanted

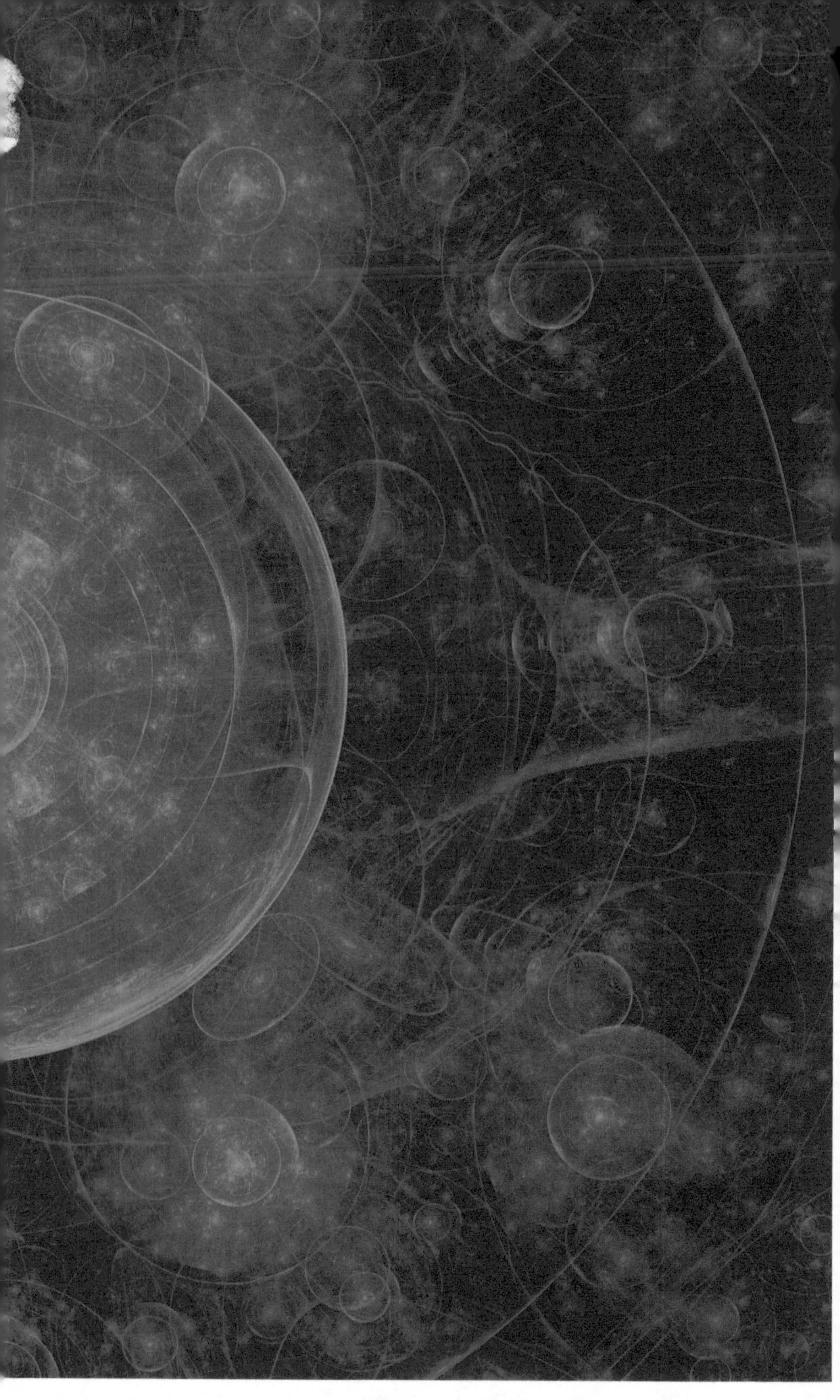

CHAPTER 1

- TUESDAY, OCTOBER 14, 1924 -

Tommy Rindell finished mopping up the floor in the dining room of Meyer's Place after closing. He was grateful that Levi had hired him at the restaurant, but it wasn't Tommy's favorite job he'd ever had. Still, the money was okay, especially when Levi pulled him from the kitchen when one of the waitresses called in sick.

Not that that happened often.

Rolling the mop bucket back into the cleaning closet, Tommy did a once-over in the kitchen to make sure everything was cleaned and ready for the breakfast rush in the morning.

"Go on and get out of here," Levi said from behind

LURED BY MAGIC

him. He was counting bills at the bar, but glanced up and smiled at Tommy. "You've had a long enough day as it is."

Tommy flashed a smile. "You sure?"

"Positive. Have a good night. See you tomorrow." Levi turned his attention back to the cash.

Tommy grabbed his coat from the rack and set out toward the trolley line.

It was late, but he was usually able to catch the final ride out. Sometimes, if Levi needed extra help after closing, Tommy had to walk all the way home. Even with a quick pace, it still took him about an hour.

Luckily, today was not one of those days.

As Tommy got on the trolley and paid the fare, he counted the rest of the cash in his wallet. There wasn't much, and payday didn't come until the end of the week. Even if Levi let him out on time the rest of the week, there was no way Tommy would be able to afford to take the trolley every night. Not if he wanted to eat too.

Ever since his father had passed away from the influenza epidemic the year before, the weight of the household finances fell on Tommy's shoulders. And he didn't have much. A modest house on the outskirts of town. His mother had run out on them right before his father became ill, so now it was just Tommy left to take care of everything.

And there wasn't any inheritance to speak of. His father could barely rub two pennies together himself. It was one of the reasons Tommy needed to quit school and start working. They needed the money. But after his father went and died on him, Tommy was back to a single-income household. Even though he was a family of one, it still cost a certain amount to maintain his modest lifestyle. An amount that Tommy could barely keep a handle on.

The trolley dropped him off at the corner of W 26th and Raspberry Streets. His house was only a short walk from there.

After the trolley pulled away, the darkness of the night truly set in. The city had yet to install streetlights in his developing neighborhood, leaving the few dim houselights the only illumination to guide him. Even the moon was hidden behind the clouds.

At the crossroads of W 27th and Raspberry, Tommy stared in the direction of the intersection. There was a shadow there, but he couldn't make out quite what it was. He began to turn to head to his house, but terrifying thoughts filled his mind.

What if it's an animal that wants to jump me?
What if it's a murderer who wants to kill me?
What if it's someone in trouble who could use my help?

"He-Hello?" he called out nervously. "Is somebody there?"

The shadow moved again, only this time Tommy's eyes were blinded as a torch lit up in flames in her hand.

She wore a dark robe and had a set of skeleton keys hanging from the arm opposite the torch. And she was beautiful, with dark hair framing her porcelain face and eyes that seemed to see right through to his soul.

"Who are you?" he asked. "And why are you standing in the middle of the road? You're going to get hit."

"Do you need help?" she asked.

Tommy's brow furrowed. "Me? I was just walking home. Are you stuck? What's going on?"

She smirked. "No, I'm not stuck."

"Then why are you in the middle of the street?"

"It's the in-between," she explained. "I assure you, it's not as dangerous as it seems."

Tommy studied her, not sure what to make of her. He considered ignoring her and walking off to his house. But that was rude. He may have been poor, but he was always polite. And what if she wished him harm? Did he really want to lead her right to his meager home? But she was just a woman. Surely, she wasn't capable of hurting anyone.

"Come here." The skeleton keys on her wrist jangled

as she raised her arm out toward him, her hand extended in his direction.

Tommy considered her command. He could just go home and pretend that none of this had happened. She would be gone in the morning. He could forget about it then.

But a bigger part of him wanted to go to her. Wanted to talk to her. Maybe more. He craved true human connection. And maybe a stranger in the street was just the person to help him with that.

Hesitantly, he stepped out into the intersection toward the woman. His eyes darted left, then right, looking out for any vehicles that might come racing by in the darkness. None came. The night was eerily still. Like they were frozen in time.

When he was in front of her, she reached up and stroked his cheek. She tutted her tongue three times. "Aw, I know you've been having a hard time lately. So lonely. Struggling to keep your head above water. No one to lean on."

"How do you—do I know you?"

"I knew your father."

His eyes grew wide. "You did? How? From where?" A young, attractive woman would've certainly come up at some point if his father had crossed paths with her.

"He was down on his luck not that long ago, either,"

she went on. "A dark place. I helped him out."

"Helped him out how? He never mentioned you."

She smiled. "As he promised he would. Your father and I made a deal. He was desperate and agreed to my terms."

"What terms?"

"I helped him have an easier life in return for payment after he died."

"You mean, like —"

"His soul," she cut in.

"You took his soul?"

She smirked. "It was the term he agreed to. Haven't you ever wondered how he always managed to have food on the table, even when he was between jobs? Or how he would always get a job offer, right after he quit one?"

"That was *you*?" Tommy couldn't believe it. Was this a dream? He was tired enough to believe that it might be. Maybe he would wake up in the morning with no recollection that any of this happened. Maybe he was imagining it, desperate to have some sort of respite to his tiring life.

"I'm capable of anything, for the right price," she went on. "Your father was desperate and I helped him. Now, the question is: are you desperate enough to agree to the same terms?"

Chapter 2

"So what exactly are we looking for?" Levi asked Evelyn as they came up to the intersection of W 27th Street and Raspberry Street. Night had fallen and the chilly fall breeze blew the crunchy leaves across the dirt road.

She squinted in the darkness. "I'm not exactly sure. My vision was murky."

"So then why are we here?" Frankie asked from her other side.

"All of my divination readings said that something bad happened at this corner."

"Which one?" Levi pointed. "There are four corners here. Were they on the sidewalk?"

She shook her head. "No. In the street."

"How can you tell?" Frankie asked. "It's so dark. Would it kill them to put in some streetlights?"

"This far out from town?" Levi commented. "Why would they?"

Frankie laughed. "Where I come from, this is damn well near the center of town."

"Don't even start with the whole 'I'm from the future' bit," Levi said with a groan.

"Would you both be quiet?" she snapped. "We're not going to be able to hear anything if you keep talking."

"Evelyn, look around!" Frankie gestured toward the intersection. "There's nothing here. And unless you have something concrete from your vision to go on, then I think we're just wasting our time."

The oracle wasn't convinced. "I just have a feeling…"

Frankie sighed and decided to give her break. He knew very well that nagging magical intuition feeling. He stepped out into the intersection and looked around, trying to find any remnants of the supernatural thread that Evelyn had picked up on.

The biggest thing that he noticed was that the area felt familiar to him. The newly-built house on the corner was his first sale as a realtor in 1984. How strange it was to see it at its infancy.

But there was something else. Underneath the familiarity. Something big that was hiding. Subdued. As if someone else didn't want the enormity of it to be found out.

"What is it?" Levi asked from beside Frankie. He hadn't seen him approach in the darkness.

The witch nodded. "I agree with Evelyn. There's a supernatural presence here. A dark one, at that."

"I told you," Evelyn said.

Levi looked between the two of them. "How do you know?"

"I can feel it," Frankie said. "The same thing Evelyn's picking up on."

Levi raised his eyebrows. "I don't feel anything."

"That's because you're nonmagical," Frankie explained. "You don't have the magical intuition the rest of us do. The one that picks up when something is just a bit off. Which is exactly how certain evils operate. They take advantage of the nonmagical who can't sense magical dangers themselves."

"It's like a sixth-sense," Evelyn added. "If the power is great enough, sometimes we can sense the magical workings happening around us. Or, in this case, what had previous transpired."

"And if they're really skilled — or if we're not seeking it out — even we can miss it ourselves." Frankie looked over at Evelyn. "That's why I didn't immediately pick up on it, either."

"Okay, so then what exactly are you guys *feeling*?" Levi asked.

Both Frankie and Evelyn said nothing, but looked around the dark, quiet, chilly neighborhood.

Finally, Frankie turned to Evelyn. "Do you think you can get a vision to recall anything that happened here?"

"I can try, but from what I can tell, there's something blocking my power." Still, she crouched to the ground and held her hands out to the dirt road, where the two streets intersected. She closed her eyes and concentrated, sitting quietly for a long time. Then, after several moments of fierce determination, she rose to her feet and shook her head.

"Nothing?" Frankie asked.

"I just feel a bad presence," she explained. "I couldn't call up a vision."

"So does that mean that everything's fine?" Levi asked.

Frankie and Evelyn exchanged more looks between them.

"That's…not necessarily the case," Frankie said.

"Sometimes there's a magic stronger than mine that is able to block my psychic interferences," Evelyn said.

"Someone is actively trying to hide whatever happened here."

"But you got the first vision unprompted," Levi said. "Back at the restaurant."

"That must've been before the protections were placed."

The trio fell silent as they looked around the darkness.

"So what do we do next?" Levi asked.

"We need to start digging," Frankie said.

"For clues?"

He shook his head. "Yes. In the ground."

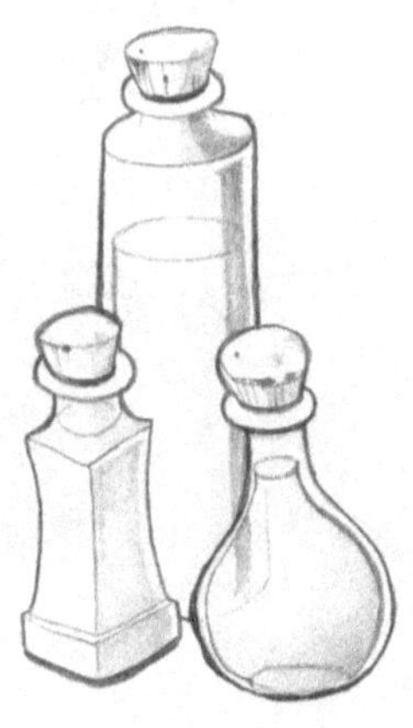

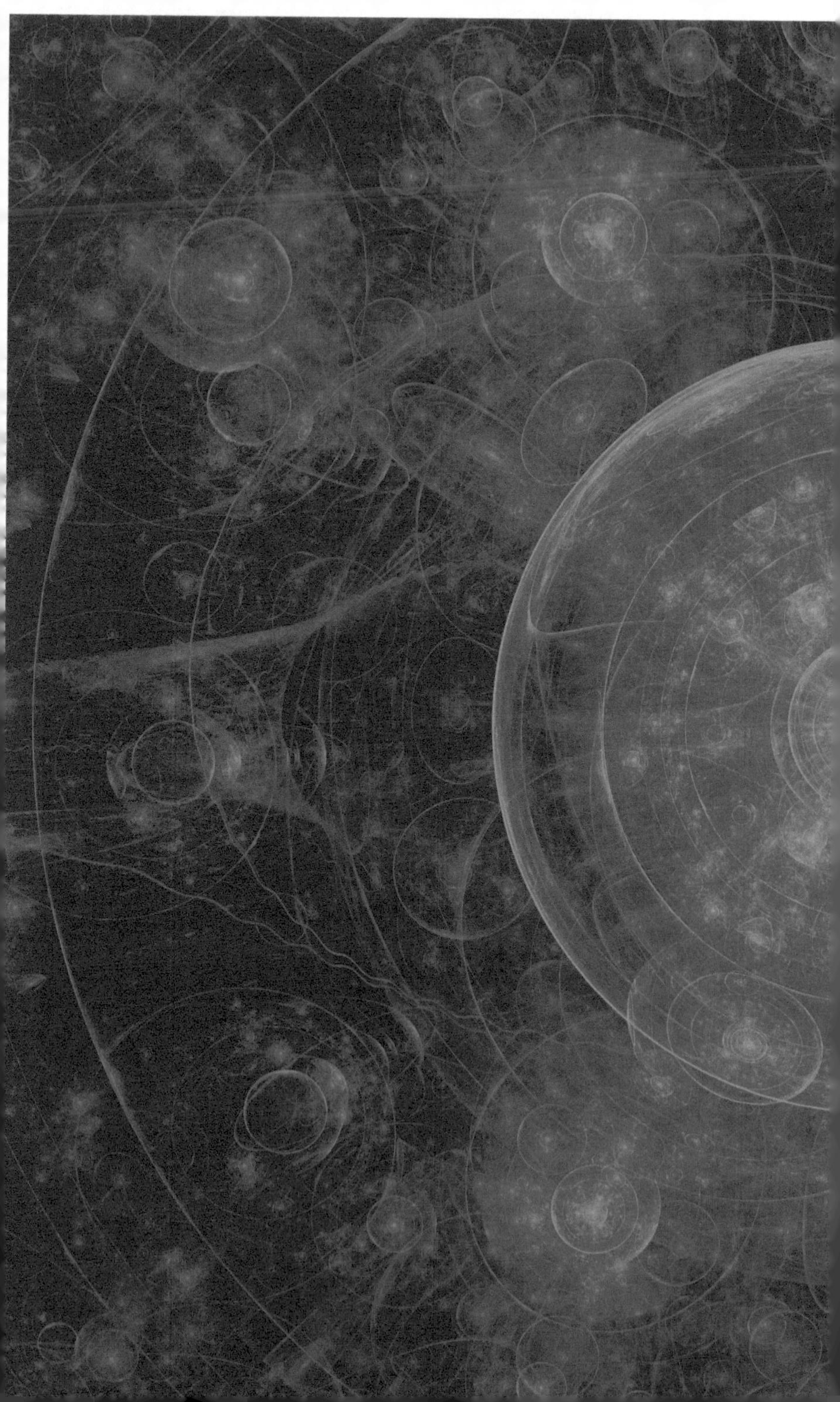

CHAPTER 3

Eddie McDonald parked on W 27th Street and walked to the front porch of his house, which was on the corner with Raspberry Street. He was exhausted, having worked ten hours at the rail yards doing mostly manual labor. The idea of a cold beer sounded like heaven.

Although, truth be told, he had been trying to have as little alcohol as possible. It didn't help his mental state any and, after his wife had left him, he hadn't been doing so hot.

Home was no comfort. He and his wife had bought the house as a starter house in their third year of marriage. Eddie had been anxious to get out of the cramped apartment that they lived in downtown. Judy, on the other hand, seemed a little disinterested in the idea of buying a house.

That should've been his first clue that something was wrong in their marriage. Of course, in the moment it was hard to tell.

Now, a year after they had bought the house together, he was a single homeowner struggling to pay the mortgage. He somehow made it every month, but it was always a close call. At the very least, the small house didn't seem too big for one person. If they had bought a bigger house with the intention of starting a family, only to be divorced a year later, that would've been a bigger sting.

Not that that was any consolation.

When Eddie put his weight on the bottom step of the porch, he heard the familiar sound of the wood squeaking. He sighed, telling himself that he'd have to fix that sometime. It was the same thing he'd been telling himself since he and Judy had first looked at the house.

The problem was, Eddie knew it was a simple fix. The board was too loose. The screws holding it in place were rusty from being in the elements year-after-year. But the idea of doing yet another job after a long day's work was impossible. And the weekend? Forget it. He needed the full two days to recharge.

Inside, Eddie tossed his keys on the kitchen table, set his lunch box on top of the fridge, and went to the sink to wash his hands. It was the same routine he had every day. His hands were always filthy from everything he had needed to get into throughout the day.

As he dried them, the stillness of the empty house nearly swallowed him up. He went to the thermostat and turned up the heat a little, just to hear the furnace running to drown out the silence. He considered the radio, but the last thing he needed was to be screamed at by the hair bands. And talk radio with their annoying DJs and endless commercials was not anything he'd ever consider putting on himself.

He went to his bedroom and changed his clothes into something cleaner — and more comfortable — then took a seat in his usual chair in the living room. He reached for the newspaper that lay on the floor beside his chair and tried to get into the front page story.

The only thing he could hear was the ringing in his ears from the silence. The thought of the cold beer in the fridge haunted him. He needed to stop drinking, or else he'd end up a drunk like his father had been. Just because Eddie was divorced didn't mean he needed to continue the cycle of alcoholism that had been in his family for years.

Giving up on the paper, Eddie tossed it aside and rose

from his chair. The damn board on the front step would at least be a distraction. It would give him something to do before he had to make himself a measly dinner and go to sleep for the night. Yet another mundane routine he performed day-in and day-out.

In the basement, he gathered the tools he needed, then went out the front door and got to work on the step.

He tried the electric screwdriver, but the rusted nail broke before he could get it out far enough. Reaching for the crowbar, he pried the step up, relieving the tension and stress in his shoulders from the physical exertion.

The board came off cleanly. Eddie grabbed his hammer and was about to pound out the rest of the rusted nails, but stopped when he noticed a folded piece of paper tucked into the space beneath the board.

The page had yellowed with age. Dirt stains and water marks spotted the paper from the rain and the snow, but it was still intact.

Carefully, Eddie lifted it and unfolded the piece of paper. There was a handwritten letter that was dated October 17, 1924. Almost sixty years ago to the day.

What was most alarming, however, was that the letter was signed by a man who Eddie knew. The very same realtor who had sold him the house.

Frankie Walker.

CHAPTER 4

The good thing about being on the outskirts of the city in the 20s was that the roads were still unpaved. Sure, it was a challenge to dig through the packed dirt, but it was a lot easier than digging through pavement.

"For the record, I really don't like the idea of digging up the middle of the road," Levi told Frankie for the fourth time since they had started digging.

The witch nodded. "I'm aware. Keep going."

"What are we actually looking for?"

"A talisman or an amulet. Maybe even a hex bag. Something that would disrupt Evelyn's power."

"And you think it's buried here?" Levi tossed another

clump of dirt to the side. They had a small hole dug, although it wasn't very deep. Maybe only a few inches.

"Positive," Frankie said. "This is the source of the disruption. Evelyn and I both felt it last night."

After they had left the corner of W 27th Street and Raspberry Street the night before, Frankie had told Levi that he wanted to get an early start the next morning. As in, before the sun came up. They couldn't risk harming anyone who might drive by with the hole they were digging. Or risk the police being called on them. And Frankie didn't want to wait any longer to see what was causing the psychic block for Evelyn.

She had decided to stay back at the speakeasy, where she felt most centered, and see if she could draw up a vision that would help clarify the mystery around her previous vision and who might be blocking it.

Levi drove his shovel into the ground again. "I really don't like this. The sun is coming up. People are going to start noticing the two of us digging in the middle of the street."

"Hush up. We'll be fine."

"Easy for you to say," Levi grumbled under his breath. "You might not be around to serve out your prison sentence."

Frankie focused his attention on digging so he didn't have to meet Levi's eyes. "It doesn't look like I'll be able to return to my time at all, so I have just as much at stake as you do."

Levi didn't respond. He, too, focused his attention on digging.

A tense silence fell between them. As the two of them continued to expand the hole, a car drove by and slammed on its horn as it passed.

Frankie ignored the car. They were now a few more inches into the ground. If they didn't find something hidden soon, then he would have to concede to the fact that he might've been wrong about his assumption.

Levi drove his shovel into the ground again and they heard a hollow thud. Both of them looked at each other before dropping to their knees and pawing at the dirt with their hands.

"What do you think it could be?" Levi piled dirt against his legs.

"Doesn't look like an amulet or a talisman. Those are typically like jewelry."

"It looks like it's a box. Do you think that has anything to do with it?"

"Possibly. It could have herbs, charms, anything. Maybe sacrifices, depending on the spell that was cast. It's hard to say."

"Are we going to uncover something bad?"

Frankie wedged the box out from the ground.

"We're about to find out."

Before Levi could stop him, Frankie opened the top of the box and peered inside. There were trinkets—some of them had supernatural connections, likely talismans—as well as tributes—portraits of people, stained with water marks.

"What is it?" Levi asked.

"Nothing good."

"What are you doing?" The voice behind them—a woman's—made the two men jump.

Levi spun around to face her and nearly fell back on the ground when he met her eyes.

Frankie turned to the woman. She held a torch in one hand and skeleton keys on a chain with the other. "You're a crossroads demon."

CHAPTER 5

The bell above the door to the Apothecary rang when Eddie stepped inside. He had never been in this shop before, although he had noticed it several times while he sat at stoplights on his way home from work. It had always caught his attention, with the white eyeball printed in the window, surrounded by a floral circular design, above which read the store's name. The lights and glittering crystals in the window called out to invite people inside.

By the look of it, the Apothecary was an occult shop. They sold things—and probably believed in things—that made Eddie uncomfortable with his Christian upbringing. But the letter he had found talked about a spell that needed a ritual to go along with it. One that he knew would not be condoned if he had gone to his regular church. The Apothecary was the only place to go to learn more about what was written in the letter.

"Good afternoon," the shop owner said. He was a scrawny old man with a black sweater hanging on his thin frame. His wiry gray hair stood up on end in the back and his glasses sat askew on his face. "Let me know if I can help you find anything."

Eddie nodded, then looked around and took in the shop. It had a certain aroma that he couldn't quite place. A mixture of natural substances—almost like dried leaves—as well as wax and something that Eddie couldn't quite place. Some sort of incense.

Various charms and trinkets hung from displays around the small shop, as well as polished colorful stones in wicker baskets on the shelves. Near the back was a small bookshelf with hardcover books that had titles written in ornate script. Eddie didn't even want to know what those books contained.

Moving on from his survey of the shop, he stepped to the counter and took a deep breath.

"I have an odd request," he started.

The old man chuckled. "Well, you're in the right place for odd things. What seems to be on your mind?"

Eddie reached for the letter in his pocket and slowly

unfolded it. "You see, I was fixing the steps to my front porch yesterday and I found this note—a letter, really. It talks about this…*spell*, I guess. It says I'm supposed to find ingredients to perform the spell properly and when to cast it." As he spoke the words out loud, he felt like a total fool for even entertaining the idea. "Anyway, I wouldn't have paid it much mind, but…well, it's written by someone I know—or knew—and it's dated 1924."

The old man was puzzled. From the magnetic clip on his shirt, Eddie saw that his name was Paul. Such an ordinary name for such an extraordinary shop.

"Is that the letter there?" Paul asked.

Eddie nodded and slid it across the counter to him.

Paul lifted his glasses so he could read the letter with his own two eyes. He held the tattered paper close and squinted as he read.

When he was finished, Eddie looked up at him. "So? What do you think? Is this a legitimate thing?"

"Well, it's a genuine spell, as far as I can tell." He took off his glasses and chewed on the end for a little bit as he studied the letter some more. "You're not, by any chance, um…*gifted*, are you?"

Eddie's eyebrows scrunched together. "Gifted?"

"As in, um…how do I put this…?"

"Are you talking about, like, magical powers or something?"

Paul's eyes lit up. "Exactly!"

Eddie shook his head vigorously. "No. Not at all. I'm completely normal. Or human. Or…whatever."

"Hmm." Paul studied the letter some more with further concentration.

"Does that matter?" Eddie thought that Paul was nuts for even asking the question, but then again wasn't Eddie nuts for *answering* the question? Everything about the letter was far from normal.

"It's just that, typically the nonmagical can't cast spells—they don't have magic in any sense," Paul explained. "However, in certain circumstances, if the conditions are right and their intentions are true, even the nonmagical can tap into the supernatural world and aid in a spell. But they can't perform one on their own."

"Oh." So it was probably harmless. Perhaps even a joke.

"You said you know the person who wrote this?"

"Sort of. He, uh, sold me my house last year. But we're not exactly *friends*."

Paul looked down at the letter again. "This letter is dated 1924."

"I know."

The old man's eyes scrutinized him. "Is that an error?"

"Not that I can tell. Look how old the paper is."

Eddie noted the irony of having an occult shop owner question *his* validity.

Paul studied the tattered paper. "I suppose you're right. But…" He let out a heavy sigh. "Well, have you checked to make sure that he's really gone? Maybe this letter was written on his behalf. Or maybe the date was simply an error."

Eddie nodded slowly, hoping that the old man was right. Hopefully this was all a misunderstanding.

"But if he did truly write this," Paul went on, "then maybe he can clarify the need for assistance—or put your mind at ease if the problem has already been resolved."

"But then why was it under my porch?"

The old man slid the paper back across the counter. "That's a question I can't answer. My own personal advice would be to go visit him. If nothing else, you can ask his daughters."

Eddie was struck by the knowledge Paul had of Frankie's daughter until his eyes skimmed over the part in the letter where Frankie mentioned them. "But the letter says to keep them out of it."

"If it's that important, then I think your friend—or acquaintance, if that's what he is—would welcome the intrusion."

Eddie looked down at the letter again. He was

hesitant to visit Frankie. He knew where he lived, sure, but he had never been there on a social call. Always for business. And that was only because their schedules didn't align to meet him at his office to sign the papers for the closing.

"I'd rather not get involved in any family drama, if that's what this is," Eddie said. "Frankie's daughters are teenagers. The last thing I want is to be thrown in jail for stalking a couple of underage girls." He shook his head. "Frankie has my phone number. If he needs my help, he can call me like anyone else."

Paul shrugged. "If that's truly the way you feel." He turned to continue unboxing his latest shipment behind the counter.

Eddie stayed where he was and stared at the letter. He was debating what to do with it. It seemed like a scam. Like a joke. But what if it wasn't? And what if there was a reason Frankie had put the note in his porch and not given him a quick ring?

"Would this spell—or any of the ingredients—be *harmful* to anyone?" Eddie asked quietly.

Paul shook his head. "Not that I can tell. However, if you're unsure of what exactly you're doing, then it might be best not to cast the spell at all. Magic is not something to be messed with hastily."

Magic, Eddie thought. *What a load of crap.* But then,

the old man was helping him out, so he decided to play nice.

Eddie nodded. "Yeah, that makes sense."

When he didn't move, Paul gave him a smile and turned his attention back to Eddie. "Would you like me to help you find those ingredients? Just in case you decide to cast the spell?"

Eddie debated for a while. "Yeah. Just in case."

CHAPTER 6

"What's a crossroads demon?" Levi looked over to Frankie for an explanation.

"Actually," the woman spoke up before Frankie could, "I'm a goddess, not a demon. My name is Hecate. Perhaps you've heard of me?"

Frankie kept his eyes locked on Hecate. "She's a disgraced goddess. When the ancient Greeks stopped worshipping her, she lost a lot of her power. Now, for all intents and purposes, she's nothing but a *demon*."

Hecate scoffed and rolled her eyes.

"And because she's basically a demon, she's stuck doing crossroads deals," Frankie told Levi. "And my guess is, she's pretty bitter about her fall from grace."

"Excuse me," she snapped. "Were you there? Have we ever met before? You don't know the whole story!"

"What part did I get wrong?" Frankie challenged.

Hecate lifted her hand that held the skeleton keys and examined her nails. "That's neither here nor there."

"Okay, will *someone* explain to me what's going on?" Levi pointed at Hecate. "If she's a demon, then she's bad, right?"

Frankie kept his eyes on the disgraced goddess. "Very bad."

"What do you want?" Hecate snapped. "I didn't come to you myself. You sought me out."

"A friend of ours had a vision about something bad happening here at this corner," Frankie started.

"So you decided to call up the forces of a goddess to—"

"*Former* goddess," Frankie corrected.

She rolled her eyes. "Either way, you decided to track me down simply to entertain your friend's déjà vu?"

"Our friend is an oracle," Levi corrected.

"So it's not like she just made up this whole scenario in her mind," Frankie added. "Besides, you showed up when I pulled the box out of the ground. And that means that there is value in the vision she had here."

"Well, if she had a vision, then why do you need me to answer any questions? Shouldn't you be talking to your friend about all of this?"

"There's something blocking her power from getting a full picture," Frankie said. "Something bad."

The witch and the fallen goddess met each other's eyes with fierce intensity, both of them sizing the other up.

"What are you trying to hide?" Frankie asked.

Hecate returned her focus to her nails. "I'm sure I don't know what you're talking about."

Frankie's fingers squished the tribute box tighter in his hands as his anger flowed through him. "Look, if you want to play games, we can play games. I'll find an exorcism that'll send you straight back to hell, no matter if you have anything to do with this or not."

Hecate tossed her head back and laughed. "Oh, please! As you've pointed out, I'm doing crossroads work now, which means that *I* control the gates of hell. If you send me to hell, it would be nothing for me to simply open the gate and allow myself to come back to this world." She smirked at him. "Nice try at a threat, sweetheart. Next time, do your homework."

The witch felt embarrassment flow through him, but it was quickly overpowered by his anger.

"Then what are you doing?" he demanded. "What

are you trying to hide?"

"What makes you think I'm hiding anything?" she insisted.

"Why else would you be here?" Levi asked.

Hecate raised her eyebrows at him. "I'd be mindful of the company you keep, young man. Associated with the likes of us could get you in trouble."

"Enough with the condemnations. Answer the damn question!" Frankie's fingers broke through the top of the tribute box, which caused Hecate to clutch at her chest.

"Easy with that!" She held out her free hand and the box flew out of Frankie's grip and right into her possession. With another flick of her hand, she magically placed it back in its resting place in the ground and the hole covered with dirt again. When her eyes returned to Frankie's, they were black for only a second.

"You don't want to touch that again," she warned. "You have no idea what you're getting yourself into."

Before Frankie and Levi could do anything more, she disappeared in a puff of black smoke.

CHAPTER 7

"Hey! Be careful with that candle, lady!" From the bar, Dennis shot Evelyn a look in the basement speakeasy of Levi's restaurant.

She glared at him, but quickly turned back to her work. She had just finished meditating and was not about to let some offhand comment uncenter her.

Dennis had been the bartender at the speakeasy for as long as Evelyn had been using it as her place to conduct her readings. Through the years she had brought in candles, herbs, incense, cards—whatever was necessary to perform the divination. Dennis was a skeptic, and one who voice his opposition at every new thing Evelyn brought in. And yet, she knew that if the chips were down, he would have her back.

Placing the white candle on the table in front of her, Evelyn pulled an ornately painted ceramic bowl from her bag near her feet and placed that on the table as well. Again reaching from her bag, she dug out some mandrake and sprinkled it into the bowl. Then, grabbing the candle, she dripped the melted wax into the bowl over the herb as she recited:

> *Guiding spirits, come to me.*
> *I ask you now to hear my plea.*
> *What darkness hides, I cannot see.*
> *Allow the scene to come to me.*

The speakeasy surrounding her faded to black. The next thing Evelyn knew, she was upstairs in the kitchen. The room was bustling as they tried to prepare for the morning breakfast rush. The kitchen manager took the lead, telling the young man working the skillet to put on another round of eggs. Meanwhile, the dish washer stacked the clean dishes back on the shelves, within reach for when the cooks finished. Waitresses came and went through the swinging doors, calling out orders as they came.

Evelyn wasn't sure who exactly she was supposed

to follow, but she was patient. As was the case with a lot of her visions, if she gave it time the truth was always revealed. In this particular case, she felt a draw from someone in the room. Like a physical force pushing her in a certain direction.

It took a few minutes of watching the kitchen staff work, but she finally pinpointed that the person who drew her to this vision was the young man at the skillet. She had met him only once before, but she couldn't quite remember his name. It was something like—

"Tommy!" the managed bellowed. "How're those hash browns doing? You keeping an eye on them?"

That was it. Tommy.

"Yes, sir," he said. "They're just about done."

"Grab a plate and throw them on," the manager said. "I've got the rest of this plate ready to go and I want it all hot when the girls serve it."

There was nothing particularly captivating about Tommy. Nothing that stood out to Evelyn as something to watch for. No hidden resentment or anger that seemed to be bubbling under the surface. There was a sense of timidness to him that could put him in danger of being a target, but what young adult didn't have the same attributes? Even Levi, who she guessed was only a few years older than Tommy, had his own brand of shyness. And he had experienced things most people couldn't even dream up.

The kitchen door swung open and Evelyn was surprised when one of the waitresses passed *through* her. Then again, if this was a vision, then that made sense.

Except, it didn't *feel* like a vision. Everything felt very real. She reached down and touched the cold surface of the stainless steel countertop, feeling the goosebumps prickle up and down her arm as she did.

No, this wasn't a vision. But then, what was it? Because none of the kitchen staff seemed to notice her. And the way the waitress stepped right through her without even a look in her direction, meant that she was connecting with Tommy in a different way. A psychic connection, but one that transported her to a different plane other than the one she normally occupied. One that was a thin veil over the real world.

She wondered how she ended up in the alternate plane when her intention—as well as the spell she had cast—did not specify removing her from the world that she belonged to. Something had gone wrong.

Or someone had interfered.

Maybe whatever spell that blocked Evelyn's vision of the crossroads also somehow redirected her spell and sent her to this alternate plane. And if that was the case, then whoever they were dealing with was very powerful.

Tommy worked through the breakfast rush before he was relieved for a few hours. As he walked toward the back door to exit into the alley, Evelyn tested a theory she had been thinking of as she watched him work.

What if she forced them apart? Would the psychic connection break, thus sending her back to her own plane?

She planted her feet on the ground and refused to move as Tommy walked further away from her. Except, the magic didn't work exactly like she thought. Tommy was calling the shots and Evelyn was forced to follow. The further he got from her, the more she felt an invisible force push her to follow him. Reluctantly, her feet moved and she was forced to keep up with him.

Down on 12th Street, Evelyn had barely enough time to jump on the trolley as it took off. It was disorienting to think about being able to pass *through* people, but luckily she could. If not, then there would be no room for her on the busy trolley.

As the trolley rolled out of town, making many stops along the way, Evelyn noticed a shadow lurking near Tommy's seat. When he got off at his stop, it followed, not seeming to pay any mind to Evelyn trailing behind.

Tommy lived around the corner from the corner Evelyn had seen in her partial vision the night before. His proximity to that corner meant something, but

LURED BY MAGIC

Evelyn couldn't figure out what. And the idea that they hadn't yet identified the person powerful enough to block her visions was frightening.

Once inside Tommy's house, he went to the bedroom and began to undress out of his white kitchen uniform. Evelyn hung back in the living room, giving him some privacy. At least she was able to give him some space.

She looked around. The house was drab. Simple. Nearly completely unfurnished. While it wasn't dirty, it wasn't clean, either. To a degree, it looked like nobody lived there at all. Cobwebs littered the corners. Dust and dead bugs lined the windowsills.

Right away, Evelyn figured that Tommy worked so much that he didn't have time to clean even his own house. Then again, it occurred to her that Tommy seemed to always be working at Meyer's Place.

"Dad? What are you—how is this…?"

The sound of Tommy's voice drew Evelyn into the bedroom, no matter what he may or may not have been wearing. As it turned out, he had already changed his clothes before he started speaking.

But there wasn't anyone else in the room with them. Tommy faced the corner, where the shadow from the trolley lingered. The longer she stared, however, the more it took the shape of an older man, one who looked strikingly similar to Tommy himself.

"You're the reason I'm dead," the shadow said. "I traded my soul so you could have a modest life and now look what you've done with my sacrifice."

Tommy looked heartbroken. "Dad. I'm sorry. I'm doing the best I can, but there just wasn't anything you left me to keep up with the bills and—"

"This isn't *my* fault," the shadow roared.

Traded his soul? Evelyn wondered to herself. If that were the case, then perhaps they were they dealing with a crossroads demon? The first vision she had *was* at the crossroads of two streets only a few houses away.

And if they *were* dealing with a crossroads demon, that would mean that the shadow was actually a phantom, sent to drive Tommy into insanity. It needed to be stopped, before it could convince Tommy of any falsehoods.

"I gave up everything for you and you're no better off than you were when I was alive," the phantom roared.

Tommy sunk to the floor, tears welling in his eyes. "Dad. I'm sorry. I'm so sorry! I'll do better. I promise."

Evelyn's heart sank for the young man. He didn't deserve the torment. Especially when it was purely the words of the phantom and not Tommy's actual father, like he was being led to believe. But as much as Evelyn wanted to say something to stop the torment, she couldn't. Even she felt a piece of herself breaking as the phantom haunted Tommy.

There was only so much a spirit could take before it broke.

CHAPTER 8

Eddie sat at his dining room table and stared at the letter from Frankie. He had read it over and over again so many times that he could recite it without even having to look at it.

Eddie,

I know this is a strange request, but please just read through the letter. I need you to put together a spell and cast it at exactly midnight on October 17, 1984. All of the directions and ingredients are below.

- Frankie Walker

P.S. Please don't tell my daughters about this. Thank you.

LURED BY MAGIC

The list of ingredients had been fairly harmless. In truth, Eddie probably could've picked them all up from the holistic aisle at the grocery store.

It was the way in which Frankie had instructed Eddie how to use the ingredients to perform the spell that stuck out to Eddie the most. It was as if Frankie knew all about the occult. Like he had actively practiced it. Either he was into some weird stuff that he kept hidden, or this whole thing really was the world's biggest joke being played out on Eddie. He wondered if someone was peeking in his windows and having a good laugh.

Nervously, Eddie looked over his shoulder and out the window. Dusk was setting in, casting a gray, hazy hue over the whole neighborhood. But there was no one even out walking, let alone peeping in his windows. No cars passing by. The neighboring houses were dark.

He was all alone.

The postscript also stuck out to Eddie. Why wouldn't Frankie want him to tell his daughters about the letter? Sure, it made sense that he would want to protect them, but why wouldn't he ask them for help? If Frankie was involved in the occult, presumably his daughters were as well. Unless they didn't know about it. But then again, neither did Eddie. Why would he ask someone who was basically a stranger and *not* his own daughters? Something wasn't adding up.

Getting up, Eddie grabbed the phone from the wall and extended the cord to his seat at the dining room table. He stared at the number pad as he considered whether he should make the call or not.

Finally, he decided that he should and punched in the number from memory.

"Thank you for calling Erie Homes and Realty," a woman's voice said on the other end. "Our offices are currently closed. If you know your party's extension, you may dial it at any time to leave a voicemail. If not, please stay on the line to listen to the following options."

Eddie pulled the phone from his face and was about to get up to hang it up, but thought twice and returned the phone to his ear. He listened to the woman's voice list all of the real estate agents and their extensions, but Frankie wasn't listed. After being prompted with another lift of options, Eddie hit the "9" button to listen to the menu again, but Frankie's name was never stated.

Huh, Eddie wondered. *Maybe Frankie moved on to another agency. Either that, or he got his job back at the city.*

He got up and returned the phone to the cradle on the wall.

Popping open the fridge, his hand hovered over a can of beer that looked particularly tasty, but his better judgment ruled out and he chose a can of pop instead.

His teeth may rot and his belly might grow, but at

least he'd be sober to experience it.

Eddie had every intention to plop on the chair in front of the TV, but the letter sitting on the dining room table caught his eye again. It was a physical reminder of Frankie Walker.

Even though their encounter with each other had been fairly brief, the two of them had struck up a mutual respect for one another. Frankie was new to his job as a realtor, sure, but he was a dedicated family man. And he tried. Eddie respected him for that. So the thought of him needing help and possibly being separated from his daughters weighed on Eddie's mind.

Frankie had reached out for help. Eddie couldn't just ignore that.

With a sigh, Eddie nodded to himself. He had made up his mind. Whether or not this was a joke, he needed to try to talk to Frankie in person. That was the only way he was going to be able to get this out of his head.

CHAPTER 9

After the breakfast rush had died off, Frankie used the down time to take a breather at the bar. He was feeling the effects of waking up so early to venture out to W 26th and Raspberry Streets. Levi, meanwhile, fussed behind the bar, restocking glasses—which were now only used for non-alcoholic beverages—and drying whatever remnants of dishwater was still left on them.

"You know," Frankie started, "maybe I could use Hecate to my advantage."

Levi raised his eyebrows. "How so?"

"To get me back to my time."

"She has the power to do that?"

"I would imagine so," he said. "Even if she doesn't, she certainly knows someone who can. Whether they're dead or alive."

"But can you trust her?"

"Can you really trust anyone? That's how I got stuck in 1924 to begin with."

Levi nodded and slid another glass on the run below the counter. "I guess that's true. So how are you going to convince her to take you back? I mean, I'm sure you're going to stick around long enough to make sure that whatever she's covering up is taken care of before you go traipsing back to your time."

"No, I wouldn't leave you guys high-and-dry." Not only did Frankie care about his friends in the 20s, but it left a whole list of unanswered questions about what the repercussions that kind of negligence would have into the future. The one Frankie was trying to return to. He wanted to make sure the time he wanted to get back to was the version he remembered and not one that had already been altered by his presence in the past.

"So then, what's your plan to get her to help you?" Levi asked.

"I could always trade in my soul."

Levi froze and stared at Frankie. "Are you serious?"

The witch shrugged. "It's crossed my mind. But only if she agrees to take me back to my time."

"But then you'd be soulless." Levi set the glass down and gripped the edge of the bar. It was the only release he could get for his annoyance with Frankie. How could he even *think* of doing such a thing?

Frankie shrugged. "So?"

"So then it wouldn't matter whether you were home or not. You wouldn't care. You'd be completely apathetic." It took all of Levi's effort not to let the edge creep into his voice.

"Maybe."

Levi shook his head vigorously. "No. That's exactly what's going to happen. When your soul is gone, so is your humanity."

"You say this as if you have experience."

"You don't—" Levi stopped his outburst and leaned in closer to Frankie, forcing himself to speak in a whisper. "You don't have to be a witch to know what having a soul means." He sat up straighter. "This is a bad idea and you know it."

"Then what other solutions do you have?" Frankie asked. "How am I supposed to get back to 1984? To my family? We've tried to send me back there ourselves—many times—and none of it's working. I need someone else to help. I need to see my daughters again."

Levi was quiet for a second. He felt for his friend, but he still couldn't let him give up his soul. "What are your daughters going to think when you return to them, only to have them look you in the eyes and know that you're not really there?"

"They won't know the difference. Even if my soul is gone, they'll just be happy that I'm home."

"Maybe at first. But you won't be the same. Not really. Removing your soul will *fundamentally* change you. And it'll alter their perception of you. Any good times you've had with them will be tarnished by the monster who returns to them, because you'll be a different person. A shell of a man."

Frankie took a deep breath and looked away. Levi was relieved his words were finally sinking in.

Levi sighed. "I know you want to get back home. I know you miss your daughters. I know you're getting desperate. But selling your soul? Come on. You know that's not the answer. We'll find another way. Magic makes anything possible, right?"

Frankie laughed humorlessly. "If only that were true." Another sigh, then, "You're probably right. I should probably keep my soul intact. I mean, without it, how am I any different from the person we're trying to stop?"

"That's a good point." Levi picked up the next glass and resumed drying it off. "We'll find another way to get you home."

"Maybe. It's just that, even if I had lost the ability to feel something by returning home, it would mean something to my girls. It would allow me to explain to them where I've been. Help them to know that I didn't just abandon them."

Levi shook his head. "No. If you return to them as a shell of the man that you are now, what they'll have is more questions and worry, than happiness and relief. In that case, you'd be better off staying away."

Frankie shrugged. "Well, it was a thought."

A terrible one, Levi thought to himself, but decided not to voice it. Frankie didn't need more ridicule. He needed a friend he could discuss an idea with. Someone who wouldn't crucify him for the thoughts he'd had. After all, Frankie was just a man who wanted to be reunited with his family. Levi couldn't fault him for that.

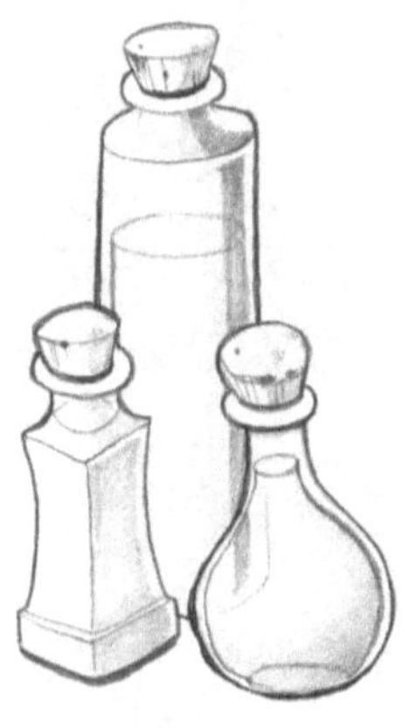

Chapter 10

Thankfully, the lunch rush was less of a "rush" and more of a "trickle." Levi, thinking about the bottom line of his business, didn't seem as thankful for that, but Frankie sure was. He was exhausted. Luckily, he only needed to carry himself up one flight of stairs to his room and then he could finally rest.

While he mostly held his own with Levi's youth, the lack of sleep was one thing Frankie's age couldn't compete with. A short afternoon nap would give him the energy he knew he needed.

The thought of going to Anna's house to ask her advice had crossed his mind, but as soon as he lay back on his bed, any thought of getting up and traveling out of town evaporated. He had the evening shift off. If he still hadn't thought of a solution for how to deal with Hecate by then, he decided that he'd go to Anna's and look through the magic book.

By now, she'd be another month pregnant with his father. The thought still boggled his mind, even though he understood the reasons it was possible. Either way, a pregnant woman should be exposed to as little evil—and stress—as possible. Frankie had been very protective of Marie when she was pregnant with the girls. It had seemed like in the two and a half years that she was having kids, the need to handle demonic situations had been muted. In hindsight, Frankie realized that was probably thanks to his parents, who likely took the brunt of it so that Frankie and Marie could have time to tend to their growing family.

Now that whole support system that Frankie had taken for granted was gone. First Marie, then his parents. Now even his girls. He was completely alone.

Getting tired of his spinning thoughts preventing him from sleep, Frankie sat up in bed and reached for a notepad on the bedside table. If he was going to find a way to figure out what Hecate was hiding—and stop whatever thing she was trying to get away with—he needed information. A direction and a plan of action for when he ultimately made it out of town to Anna's and consulted *The Art of Magic.*

On the pad of paper, he began writing down what he knew about crossroads demons, which was what Hecate was acting as now that she had lost her power as a goddess.

They operated at night time.

They tended to target desperate people who were at rock bottom.

They always appeared at a crossroads and were usually stuck there.

They first entered the mortal world through a doorway, which is opened by someone desperate enough to summon them with a sacrificial offering of some sort — just like the box that Frankie and Levi had dug up earlier that morning.

The list continued to grow as Frankie remembered more. He began to roll his head back to stretch out the kink in his neck when he saw her standing in the corner of the room.

Marie.

His wife.

Frankie shook his head and blinked, but Marie was still there. She smiled at him.

The sight of her washed away whatever fear Frankie initially had at the presence of someone else in his small hotel room. Now, he was nearly in tears, seeing her in flesh and blood. He didn't want to say anything to ruin the moment or make the sight of her disappear.

She was here. His sweet, beautiful wife.

Slowly, he scooted to the edge of the bed to rise, keeping his eyes locked on her at all times. He was afraid to blink, for fear that her image would disappear from existence in the split second his eyes were closed.

As he rounded the corner of the bed, he asked softly, quietly, "How are you here?"

Just as he feared, his words caused her image to fade. To disappear into the ether.

"Wait!" he called, before stopping himself. If he were too loud, someone from downstairs would come up and ask if he was okay. And this moment was too precious to interrupt.

But Marie was fading.

"Marie," he whispered as her figure faded completely.

Frankie dropped to his knees and felt himself overcome with sobs. The mere sight of her brought a rush of emotions and memories to the surface.

And also regrets.

While his mind was filled with the images of their wedding, their daughters being born, and quiet evenings at home, he was also bombarded with questions: why couldn't she have lived longer? Why did she have to die?

Where would they be if she had lived? What if it had been him instead?

Sitting back on his heels, Frankie let the tears spill. He cast one last look to the corner where Marie had been standing, and then used the bed frame to haul himself to his feet.

Wiping away the moisture from his face, he made a decision: this moment was just for him and Marie. Maybe it had been her spirit coming to find him to tell him that everything would be okay. Maybe it was purely a figment of his imagination.

Either way, there was no way he was going to tell this to anyone.

CHAPTER 11

While Frankie went upstairs to rest, Levi thought that he'd better find Evelyn and inform her of everything. Not just their encounter with Hecate, but also that Frankie was considering trading in his soul for a trip back to 1984.

That thought alone was cause for concern. Levi wasn't sure if he had fully convinced Frankie that it was a bad idea, and he worried that Frankie would try to summon Hecate himself and make the deal without them knowing. And since Levi was nonmagical, it was important to bring someone else who had magic into the fold. Someone who had more experience with the supernatural who would further give credence to Levi's warnings.

LURED BY MAGIC

As Levi made his way down the secret staircase in the back room, down into the basement speakeasy, he wondered if Evelyn had had any luck with trying to see through the fog in her vision. The fact that Levi and Frankie had been back for hours and she hadn't come upstairs to tell them her findings yet suggested that she hadn't been successful.

Then again, she could've also just gotten busy with customers looking to have their fortunes told. Even Evelyn had to make a living.

The oracle had been setting up shop in Levi's speakeasy for years. She had started back when Levi's father owned the building. It was her psychic services that she sold. Everything from palm readings to tea leaves to seances. She did it all to the best of her ability. But for her mostly nonmagical clients, the theatrics she went through was enough for them to feel like they got their money's worth.

From what Levi understood, most people thought it was a fun gimmick. Something to splurge on when they were already breaking the social rules by drinking in private. And the fact that Evelyn was a true oracle meant that she could provide them with enough information to keep them coming back for more.

Even Levi had thought it was a joke. Until Frankie crashed in on a magical fight between two gangs and blew his mind with the secret supernatural world lurking under his own nose.

In the speakeasy, Levi did a quick survey of the room and was surprised that Evelyn was not seated at her usual booth. He walked over to it and saw that her bag was still tucked on the floor against the seat and an empty glass sat on the table.

She had been there.

"Hey, Dennis," Levi called to the bartender. "Have you seen Evelyn?"

"Who?" Dennis wiped up the bar with a rag. At the end, sat two gentlemen in business suits, huddled together in private conversation. No one ever spoke of what happened in the speakeasy. They were likely hashing out a business deal that they would deny publicly. Alcohol consumption was not the only secret that was kept at the speakeasy.

"The oracle." Levi pointed to the empty booth.

Dennis's eyebrows scrunched. "You mean the psychic."

"That's the one."

"What about her?"

"Have you seen her?"

"I see a lot of people."

Levi sighed heavily to show his frustration. "I'm not trying to turn her in, Dennis. I'm worried about where she is. Have you seen her?"

"I try not to stare."

"It's a yes or no question."

"I might've seen her around."

"She's here every day. I know you notice her. She comes in each day and sets up in the same booth and does psychic readings for people. Except for today."

"I think I saw her this morning."

Levi glanced back at the booth, just to confirm that it was still empty. It would be just his luck to press Dennis, only to find out that Evelyn had simply run off to the ladies' room. Turning his attention back to Dennis, he asked, "Do you know where she went?"

The bartender shrugged. "She was there, then she wasn't. I don't keep tabs on people. That's not what you pay me to do."

Levi sighed again. "Okay. Thanks. If you see her, let her know I'm looking for her."

"I'm making no promises," he offered. "I stay out of people's business."

There was no point trying to get anymore information out of him. He truly was great at his job, which required secrecy during Prohibition. But it was infuriatingly unhelpful.

Levi walked over to Evelyn's booth and ran his hands along the tabletop. These were the moments he wished he had powers too. He could help Frankie find a way back to 1984 and make sure that Evelyn was safe.

But he didn't need supernatural powers to know that something wasn't right. He might not have the ability to sense something magical going on, but he knew something was off. Evelyn had made this booth her livelihood for years, never missing a day. On good days, she made more money than Levi made with the restaurant, after expenses. There was no way she would turn that down. Not when they were still unsure of the threat level of Hecate.

And maybe this was a sign that Hecate was somehow involved. Or maybe it was completely unrelated. There were only two things that Levi was absolutely sure of. The first was that he felt frustratingly helpless. And the second was that something had happened to Evelyn.

CHAPTER 12

*I*t *was a vivid daydream*, Frankie thought to himself as he walked down State Street, bracing himself in his jacket against the cold. *Simply a product of my imagination, trying to comfort me so I don't go insane.*

The rational part of Frankie wanted to believe that seeing his late wife had been merely psychology, but the supernatural part of him knew that anything was possible. Of course, bringing someone back who'd been dead for fourteen years was never a good thing.

Then again, if they were now in 1924, that meant that Marie hadn't even been born yet, which might've played a factor in whether her appearance was a good thing or not. However, the fact that she came to Frankie as the adult she was when she died complicated things.

The simple fact was that he didn't know what was going on. All he knew was that he couldn't stand to be in the same room as where the apparition — whether real or not — had appeared. He had decided to go out for a walk to get his mind off of things. The only trouble was, he had nothing to distract his mind. No matter how far he got from Levi's place, his brain had switched to the 24-hour Marie station.

Frankie busied himself by stopping to admire all of the shop windows along State Street. The throngs of people out shopping — even on chilly, fall day — wasn't enough to take his mind off of Marie. Even as he tried to force himself to think of other things, like how different State Street looked in the twenties compared to the eighties, or how the clothing styles had evolved, or how far technology had come, all he could think about was his dead wife.

Looking through the glass into the display of one shop, he nearly fell to the ground when he saw Marie's reflection in the glass standing behind his own.

He whipped around, desperate to get another look at her with his own two eyes, but she wasn't there. Instead, there stood a short, plump lady in a thick coat and flowing dress that gave him a confused look at his behavior.

"Sorry," he murmured to her, then continued on down the street.

I'm losing my mind, he thought. *I need another distraction.*

He only had about twenty dollars in his pocket from the last time Levi paid him. Rent wasn't a consideration, being that Frankie worked so much in Levi's restaurant for room and board. But Levi always gave him something after he had paid the other employees, so Frankie had some money to spend.

The next store over was a men's clothing shop and Frankie entered. He had been meaning to get a few extra time-appropriate outfits for himself. Borrowing clothes from Levi had run its course, considering that the much-younger Levi was also much smaller than Frankie. And there were only so many clothes that Frankie could find from thrift stores and church sales.

Frankie selected a pair of pants and a collared shirt, then went to the dressing room to try them on. After he pulled back the curtain, he turned to hang his selections on the hook and was face-to-face with Marie.

He jumped back, careful not to spill out of the curtain and into the store.

"Marie?" he whispered. "Is it really you?"

She smiled at him and nodded. "It's me, Frankie." She reached out and stroked his face and he nearly melted at the warm, soft touch of her hand. The one he had nearly forgotten.

Tears welled in his eyes. "How? Why? What's going on?"

"You'll understand eventually. For now, can't we just enjoy each other's company?" She reached for him and it took every ounce of effort in him to push away from her after a moment's hesitation.

"Wait, I need to know how you got here. I need to know that you're —"

"Real?" she finished. Again, she took his face in both of her hands and planted a soft kiss on his lips. "Does this feel real?"

He reached up and gripped her hands, the tears starting to fall down his cheeks. "Oh, I've missed you so much."

She rested her forehead against his. "I've missed you too. I want us to be together again."

"We are now."

"No." She seemed to swallow a lump in her throat. "No, this isn't — I meant, I want us to really be together. This is just — this is temporary."

He pulled away from her to look her in the eyes, but held her hands. "What do you mean? What's going on?"

"Promise me we can be together, Frankie."

"You know I want us to be," he said. "Tell me how.

What can I do so that you and I never have to be apart again?"

"I think you know."

He stared into her eyes to judge if she was serious. The look she gave said that she was.

"It's the only way," she pleaded.

"But Levi said —"

"Are you going to believe a nonmagical boy you've only known for a month, or the wife you've committed your life to?" She cradled his face in her hands again. "Sweetie, do it for me. Do it for us."

Frankie shook his head. "But I don't know if I can. What about the girls? What about me? My soul? My humanity?"

"The girls have already lost you," she said. "And you've lost everything. What else is left?"

He was quiet as the impact of her words sunk in. He wanted nothing more than to wrap her in his arms and make everything okay. But was it really that simple?

"Do it, Frankie," she said. "Make the deal with Hecate."

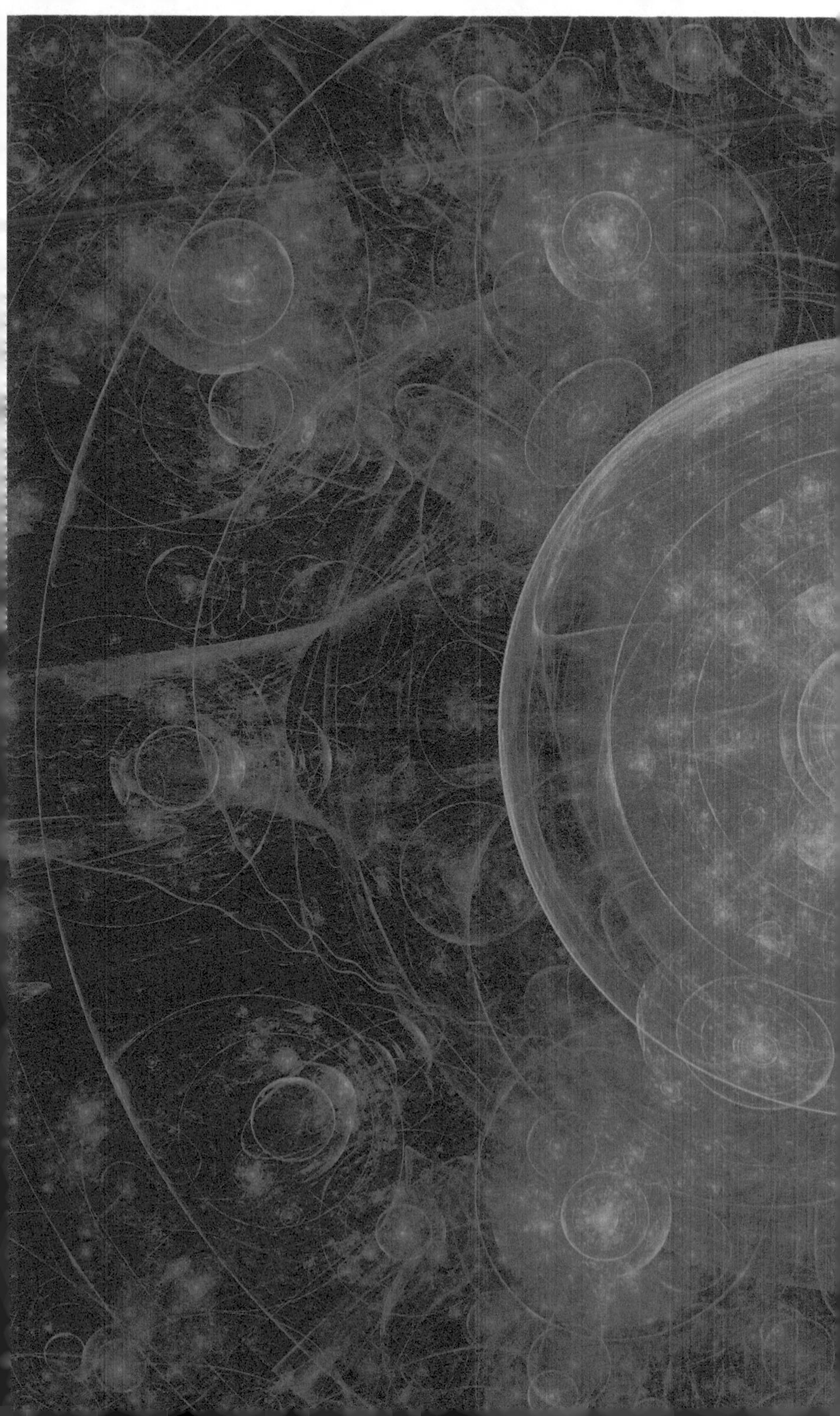

CHAPTER 13

Eddie knocked on the door of the Walker house on Arlington. He had been debating the trip all day and, even now as he stood on the doorstep waiting for an answer, he considered turning and going home and forgetting the idea altogether.

The more he looked into Frankie and the note that he supposedly left, the more confused he became. On the surface, it seemed like a prank, but what if it wasn't? And the fact that he hadn't been in touch with Frankie Walker in almost a year was odd as well.

What was worse was that Eddie had visited Erie Homes and Realty, Frankie's realty office, earlier that day and they said he didn't work for them anymore. Of course, that could mean that he simply changed jobs, but the way that everyone at the office seemed to tense up at any questions about him, and the fact that they were so vague about what had happened to his employment, left Eddie feeling like there was more to the story.

Which brought him to the Walker house. Frankie's letter explicitly said to leave his daughters out of it, but perhaps simply asking *about* him—without mentioning the letter—was a way around that promise.

The door swung open and a young woman stood on the other side. She had long dark hair, that was draped over one shoulder. She wore a black sweater that she pulled closed at the chilly breeze.

"Hi," she said timidly.

"Are you one of Frankie Walker's daughters?" Eddie had only met the girls one time and that had been over a year ago, which made a big difference with teenagers. They changed so much that it was hard to tell if she was, in fact, Frankie's daughter. For all he knew, they had moved out of Erie altogether.

She nodded. "Yeah, I'm Samantha. Who are you?"

He extended his hand. "I'm Eddie McDonald. I bought a house with your dad last year."

She shook his hand, but quickly pulled it back and crossed it in front of her. "How can I help you?"

"Well, I was hoping to talk to him. If he's in."

Samantha glanced inside the house, then turned back to Eddie. "He's not home right now."

"Oh." For a brief moment, Eddie wondered if she was lying. But the response had come so fast, so naturally, that he felt compelled to believe her. "Okay. Well. Do you know when he *will* be home?"

She shook her head. "I'm not sure."

He nodded in response. Samantha had very short, definitive answers. She was polite, but it was obvious that she didn't want to talk.

"Is there something I can help you with?" she offered.

Eddie considered that. He thought about the letter, more specifically the spell that Frankie had outlined, a thought that if Frankie had truly left it, that mean was mixed up in some kind of occult or voodoo no that Eddie wasn't comfortable getting mixed up if Frankie *was* involved in it, there was a good daughters were too. The trouble was, he di that was a good thing or not.

Finally, he shook his head. "No, I can. Thanks anyway." He began to steps. "Have your dad give me a chance."

He made it down to the si called to him from the front d

"Mr. McDonald!"

Eddie turned and looked back at her.

"Have you…have you heard from my dad lately?"

Odd question to ask, he thought. *Where the hell is he if his own kids haven't even heard from him?* Then he remembered the letter was dated 1924—if that wasn't a joke. Or maybe simply a misprint.

"No, I haven't." He thought it'd be better to tell her the truth, instead of arouse suspicion if she got the impression that he was lying. Then again, *was* he lying? The letter was a form of communication, but how could he verify that Frankie had truly been the one to leave it for him? Maybe it had been a different Frankie Walker altogether?

Samantha frowned, then waved and said, "Okay. I'll have him call you when I see him." She disappeared into the house before he could say another word.

Back at his car, Eddie got behind the wheel and reached for the letter from the passenger seat. He reread for the millionth time, again noting the date and the post-script.

Setting it aside, he shook his head as he started the and shifted it into gear. There were three perfectly possible explanations for the letter.

The first was that it was left by a different Frankie from 1924.

The second was that it was a sick prank.

And the third was that the Frankie Walker that Eddie knew had gone completely off his rocker.

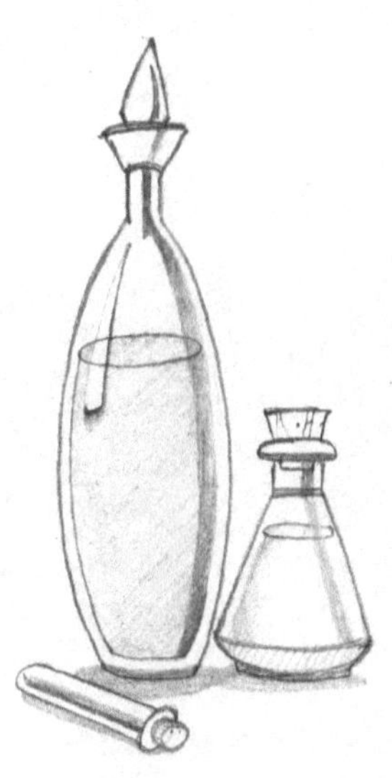

CHAPTER 14

Tommy made his way back onto the trolley for the dinner shift at Levi's. That meant that Evelyn raced to catch the trolley as well. She made it onto the vehicle, but barely.

The trolley was not her favorite way to travel, even if it was necessary for cross-town trips.

Snagging a seat on the end, Evelyn watched Tommy stare out the window across the aisle and wondered what was going on magically that put her in this situation to begin with.

It had to have been a psychic connection. That was the only solution Evelyn could come up with as to why she was now attached to Tommy. Magically, she was forced within close proximity of him, and yet he didn't seem to see her. And the only reason she was attached to him to begin with was because she had been trying to connect psychically to whatever Hecate was trying to hide.

That meant that somehow Tommy was connected to Hecate.

Okay, Evelyn thought to herself. *How am I going to break this psychic connection without breaking Tommy?*

The thought crossed her mind that if she uncovered whatever Hecate was trying to hide, then the spell Evelyn had cast would be lifted. And that much would've been true—even if it was infuriating not to be able to control where she went herself. However, this wasn't a typical psychic connection. She had had those before. This one was different.

With most psychic connections, the oracle—or psychic, soothsayer, or seer—essentially transported part of their consciousness into the consciousness of the person they were connecting with. But they still retained their hold on the real world, meaning they could exit the connection whenever they chose.

This wasn't like that at all. It was as if Evelyn had transported to a different plane to be a fly on the wall for Tommy's life.

Wait, she thought. *That's it. Somehow I transported*

myself to a different plane. And Tommy is the anchor between the two planes. But why?

The trolley stopped near State Street and Tommy went to the back to exit. Evelyn rushed to her feet and followed him out into the darkening night.

As she followed, she looked around at her surroundings with more of a critical eye. This was the same State Street that she had always remembered: bustling, with many signs and advertisements nearly shouting for the walkers to enter each retail establishment and spend lots of money.

Only, the whole outlook seemed grimmer somehow. Almost as if there were a filter placed over the world. She thought of camera film and how the depiction was the same and yet not quite right. There was always a distortion, of sorts, to the capturing of reality.

That's exactly what she was seeing with her own two eyes as she traveled through this world. She couldn't believe she hadn't noticed it before.

Tommy stepped inside Meyer's Place and the door swung in Evelyn's face as she followed. She ducked, then remembered that it didn't matter if it had hit her. She operated on a different plane, meaning that the physical rules of the world were different. When she opened the door in her plane, it wouldn't necessarily open the door in the plane that Tommy existed on. Perhaps the bell above the door may jingle a faint sound, but that'd be the only sign that she had entered.

Inside, the restaurant was busy. Luckily, the kitchen was in close enough proximity that she could sit at the end of the bar and observe the dining room while Tommy worked in the kitchen. She doubted anything magical would happen while he was helping the cook, but she still felt guilty for not keeping her eyes on him at all time.

The sight of Levi and Frankie moving about the dining room, bringing in and out orders and serving the diners brought a flicker of hope to her heart. Maybe Frankie would see her. Maybe the connection was magical. Maybe that was going to be her way out.

But as she watched Frankie, she noticed a shadow lurking behind him everywhere he went. She got to her feet and tried to step closer, but an invisible barrier stopped her: she was stepping too far from Tommy.

Instead, she studied the shadow from afar. As Frankie came back toward her to enter the kitchen, she caught a better glimpse of the shadow, which took the shape of a woman they closer they got to her. Beautiful, at first, but close-up, Evelyn saw the decay under the surface. The woman looked almost like a walking corpse.

Evelyn's heart raced as she thought of the possibilities of what it could mean. None of them were good.

CHAPTER 15

Ever since Frankie had returned to the restaurant and started working the dinner shift, he did not feel well at all. He was exhausted and in a mental fog. One so bad that he had never experienced anything like it before.

Sleep, he thought. *That's all I need.*

After Marie had encouraged him to make the deal with Hecate back in the dressing room, Frankie had some serious reservations about it and stepped out into the store to think it over. When he had turned back to the dressing room, it had been empty and Marie had been nowhere in sight.

So far, he hadn't seen her during his entire walk back to Levi's.

LURED BY MAGIC

"Frankie!" Levi called from the top of the stairs as Frankie was halfway up to his room. "There you are!"

The witch groaned and clung to the handrail as he pushed himself to climb the steps. Any amount of physical effort was getting to be too much work.

"Why are you moving so slow?" Levi asked once Frankie joined him on the second floor.

Frankie waved him off as he crossed the hall to his room. "Tired." Even speaking took a lot out of him.

"Yeah, I guess I am too. But you only have yourself to blame for that. You're the one who got us up so early so we could dig that hole in the middle of the street."

Frankie unlocked the door to his room and flopped back on his bed. It wasn't as nice as his bed from 1984, but at that point, it was heavenly after he made the trek all the way down State Street.

"Come on, sit up." Levi tugged at Frankie's arm to get him to move.

Reluctantly, Frankie obliged.

"Listen to me: Evelyn is missing."

At that, Frankie perked up. "Missing? How do you know?"

"She's not downstairs."

Frankie narrowed his eyes. "Okay…"

"And that's never happened before."

"Maybe she set up shop somewhere else."

Levi shook his head. "No. She's always been set up here. Even before I owned the place. She's been coming for *years* and hasn't missed a day."

"So maybe she went to go check in on Hecate."

"Without telling us?"

Frankie shrugged. "It's a thought."

"I'm telling you, she's missing. What's the matter with you? Why aren't you more concerned about this?"

"I don't know," Frankie responded around a yawn, then collapsed back on the bed.

"Well, sit up." Levi tugged at his arm again. "I need your help, because I think Evelyn has gone somewhere that *I* can't reach, if you catch my drift."

"You think this is supernatural?" Frankie sat up, but rubbed at his eyes.

"Maybe."

Another yawn. "She'll show up."

"That's it." With both hands now, Levi yanked Frankie by the hands and launched him up onto his feet, then guided him out the door.

"Hey, what's going on? What are you doing?" Frankie protested.

"We're going downstairs and I'm giving you coffee. You need to wake up."

It took deliberate concentration for Frankie to focus on the steps as he descended. Once he made it back down to the dining room, he sat at the bar where Levi went around back and poured Frankie a cup of coffee.

It only took one sip, but already Frankie felt better. "That helped. A little."

"Good." Levi leaned in close and lowered his voice. "Now I need you to think. Is there anything—any spell or anything—you can think of that would help us find her?"

Frankie leaned against his hand. "I don't know."

"Think, damn it!" Levi blurted. He looked around and noted the diners looking at him. He cleared his throat, then called to Tommy, who was bussing tables. "Tommy, could you get going on those dishes before the dinner rush really starts?"

Tommy nodded, then disappeared back into the kitchen with a bin full of dirty dishes.

After he was gone and the diners went back to their private conversations, Levi turned to Frankie. "Isn't there a way to call to her to bring her here?"

"Like summoning her?"

"Yeah!"

Frankie shrugged. "I could try it. I'd have to come up with a spell."

"You do that kind of stuff all the time," Levi said. "It should be easy."

As hard as Frankie tried, he couldn't think up a spell

from scratch at that moment. His brain was in too much of a fog. Too worried about the apparition of Marie.

Finally, he remembered a very rudimentary spell that one of his girls had tried when they were still learning the ways of witchcraft. It wasn't perfect—he wasn't certain it would work, or even that he was remembering it correctly, but it was all he had.

He cleared his throat and started reciting, but Levi stopped him.

"Whoa, whoa! You're doing it *here*? In front of everyone?"

Frankie shrugged. "Why not?"

"Um…because then people will see? Go in the back room, at least." Levi ushered Frankie through the door in the back and right in front of the secret wall that led down to the basement speakeasy.

"Is this better?" Frankie knew that he should care about exposure, but at the moment he was feeling so drained. Numb.

"Much better. Go ahead."

Again, Frankie cleared his throat and recited:

Bring Evelyn to this here place,
Hurry now, we have little time to waste.

Levi raised his eyebrows. "*That* was the spell?"

LURED BY MAGIC

"It's better than anything you've come up with."

"Is it?" Levi spread his arms and gestured to the empty room. "It didn't work, Frankie!"

"And this stress isn't helping!" In the corner, Frankie caught the faintest resemblance of Marie standing and smiling at him.

Make the deal, sweetie, her voice sounded in his head. *Help us be together forever.*

"What?" Levi turned to look where Frankie was looking, then turned back to his friend. "What is it? What's going on?"

"Nothing. It's nothing."

Levi turned to get another look, but something caught *his* eye. As Levi darted into the dining and toward the front door, Frankie saw it too. Standing outside the window on the street was Hecate.

CHAPTER 16

- THURSDAY, OCTOBER 16, 1924 -

Evelyn stood as far as she could from Tommy, just outside the kitchen in the dining room. She hadn't been able to hear all of Frankie and Levi's conversation, but she heard enough to know that Levi could tell that something was off.

Worse, she also saw the shadow lurking behind Frankie again. It was a phantom of some sort and it seemed to have a negative effect on him. Very much like the shadow that followed Tommy around.

The phantom near Frankie seemed to intensify and Evelyn looked around to see if there was an external force at play. That's when she noticed Hecate outside the restaurant.

Lured by Magic

"Hey!" Evelyn called to her out of reflex. She didn't expect a reaction of any kind, but to the oracle's surprise, Hecate stopped and looked at Evelyn, stunned.

The oracle tried to run at the crossroads demon, but she was kept firmly in place by her connection with Tommy.

A moment later, however, Levi burst out of the back room door and raced through the dining room toward Hecate. Frankie trailed behind, and his own phantom brought up the rear.

Evelyn ran back into the kitchen and tried to get Tommy's attention. The kitchen staff was in the midst of the dinner rush, so he was hard at work getting everything in order. Evelyn thought about focusing her energy on connecting with the physical world to get his attention, but that was a stretch. Even if she was able to somehow make a bowl clang on the counter or a cabinet slam shut, Tommy wouldn't necessarily know what that meant. And he might not even notice it in the rush. Besides, it would take a lot out of her and she already felt herself growing weaker the longer she spent on this alternate plane.

But without that, she had no other options to draw attention to Hecate, or to follow her on her own. She tried to get Tommy's attention by waving her arms in front of him. Tried stepping into his body to possess him.

Tried reaching for him, as if she were about to lay her hands on him.

None of it worked.

She was completely invisible. Untraceable. That thought alone brought a feeling of dread that Evelyn hadn't expected. Loneliness. Hopelessness.

The more she tried to get Tommy's attention, the firmer the shadow lurking near him became. Eventually, it took the shape of a middle-aged man. Once he had fully taken the shape of the man, he turned on Evelyn.

"What are you doing?" the phantom bellowed at her. "Leave my boy alone!"

The power in his voice scared Evelyn, then made her shrink back in fear. The look in his eyes and the authority he carried forced her to stop completely. Forced her to obey, as much as she didn't want to. That look sent a chill right down to her core. One that made her feel less alive, the longer he kept his eyes on her.

There was a lot that she didn't understand, but one thing she knew for certain: the longer she was trapped — the longer this mysterious negative force had to wreak havoc — the more likely it was that she was going to die.

Levi was her only hope. Hopefully he could save both her and Frankie. If not, then this was the end for them both.

CHAPTER 17

Levi rushed through the door of the restaurant and out onto the sidewalk. There were still quite a few people out shopping and running errands, despite the chilly night. Cars whizzed by on the street at the major five-point intersection near the front of the building. The commotion made him pause to get his bearings as his eyes searched the crowd and the traffic for the former goddess.

Finally, he spotted her.

Hecate weaved between the crowd on the sidewalk and Levi followed her in hot pursuit.

"Sorry," he murmured as he bumped into people. "Excuse me."

LURED BY MAGIC

"Hey!" a lady barked at him when he nearly flattened her to the ground.

"Sorry!" he called over his shoulder, but turned to keep his eyes on Hecate.

The crossroads demon darted into the street and almost collided with an oncoming car. She stopped short and the car slammed on its horn as it narrowly missed her.

"Stop!" Levi called out, even though he knew it was useless.

Hecate looked back at him and then continued the dangerous trek into the middle of the intersection where she…vanished.

Levi took one step off the sidewalk and stopped on the edge of the street. His eyes scanned the whole intersection, looking around cars, surveying the line of people on the opposite side of the street.

Hecate was nowhere to be seen.

Another car slammed on its horn and Levi jumped back onto the safety of the sidewalk as the car careened by.

Levi looked around again, but couldn't see any sign of Hecate. He had lost her. But where had she gone? One minute she was there and the next she wasn't. Levi didn't know a lot about magic, but he knew even that was odd.

But with no other choice, he turned and walked back to the restaurant.

Outside, Frankie was huddled on the sidewalk, leaning against the front of the building. He held his legs and rocked back and forth. His shoulder shook and his face was wet with tears.

"Hey, what's going on?" Levi crouched down beside his friend. He reached for his shoulder, but Frankie flinched away from him.

"My wife," Frankie blurted.

"Your wife?"

The witch nodded. "Marie."

Levi narrowed his eyes and searched his mind for the best follow-up question. "Did you…*see* her?" The math didn't make sense to Levi. From what little he knew about Frankie's late wife, she had been the same age as Frankie when they were married in the future. It was impossible for him to see her in this time.

Frankie nodded again. "Yeah. A couple times."

"Where?"

"It doesn't matter."

Levi pinched the bridge of his nose. First Evelyn went missing and now Frankie was crying over his wife, who hadn't even been born yet in this time and was dead in Frankie's time. He was feeling the strain of keeping their little trio together. "What did Marie say to you?"

Lured by Magic

This got his attention. Frankie finally met his friend's eyes. "She needs me. She needs me to join her."

"Join her?" Levi asked. "Join her where? What are you talking about?"

"In the afterlife," Frankie said. "We'll be together when I'm dead. I have to find Hecate. I have to sell my soul!"

CHAPTER 18

Levi had managed to get Frankie into the back room without too much disturbance to the diners in the restaurant.

This whole night has been crazy, Levi thought to himself. *It's a wonder any of them even come back.*

He propped Frankie against the icebox, who slumped to the floor, limp. Levi rolled his neck to try to work out some of the knots forming.

"What the hell are you talking about?" he asked blankly. "Why do you want to sell your soul?" It took all of his effort not to yell at him for it. They had discussed this already.

"I have to sell my soul," Frankie repeated. "That's the

only way I'll get to see my wife."

"Because you'll be dead?"

"Yes!"

"Okay." Levi let out a deep breath, trying to control his own anger, while also figuring out how best to help his friend. "Okay. Where did you see her? When did she tell you? Was it…in a dream or something?"

"She was standing right there!" He pointed to the corner.

Levi looked over his shoulder, but didn't see anything. His eyes lingered, but still nothing was there. "Is she standing there now?"

"Of course not. She's not here right now."

"Well, where did she go?"

Frankie shrugged. "I don't know! But that's not important. What's important is that I need to find her again. I have to be with her forever and the only way I can do that is if I make a deal with Hecate. Trade my soul for an eternity with my wife."

"And you got all of this from your wife?"

"Yes!"

Levi rubbed his forehead and sighed. "Frankie, I don't mean this to be rude, but your wife's dead."

"That's why this is the only way for us to be together!"

"And this doesn't seem at all suspicious to you?"

"No. Why wouldn't I want to spend eternity with my wife?"

Levi thought about Frankie's behavior over the course of the day. For the most part, it had seemed normal. But the exhaustion was new—Frankie seemed to be more tired than an early wake-up would warrant—and now he was seeing things. Based on Frankie's behavior outside, Levi thought it was safe to assume that Hecate was behind it.

"Okay, I need you to really think this through," Levi started. "Don't shoot it down right away. Really think about it."

"I need to see my wife!"

"I'm not talking about that. Listen, don't you think it's a little odd that the woman that *you* remember from the 70s is suddenly here? I mean, your time period is the 80s, and she was dead when you came to my time. That's a ten year difference."

"So?"

"So why would she be here? Did she cast a spell in the 70s to take her back to this moment?"

"No. She—she died."

Levi nodded and smiled. Frankie was finally getting it. "Right. That's what happened. It was terrible and tragic and you never truly got over it. Of course you want to see her, but Frankie, this isn't her. Whoever—or whatever—you're seeing is not the woman you love."

Frankie shook his head and scooted away from Levi, turning away from him. "Then maybe it was her ghost."

"In 1924? Before she was even born? I may not have magic, but that seems like a stretch, even for you."

Silence.

Levi sighed again. "Frankie, don't you think it's possible that you're being manipulated? Like I said, you never really got over her death. Someone bad, like Hecate, could be using that to their advantage. Maybe Hecate only sent Marie's image to get you off her trail. It sounds like she wants to convince you to trade in your soul. And once you do that, it's too late."

Frankie was quiet as his friend talked. But the silence meant that the gears were turning in his mind. Levi decided to hold off on saying anything else so that Frankie could warm up to the idea that what Levi was saying was the truth.

"You may be right," the witch finally admitted.

Levi smiled. "It doesn't make sense, does it?"

Frankie shook his head. "No. There's no way—natural or supernatural—for Marie to genuinely be here now. Maybe in my time her spirit could show up to communicate with me, but she couldn't come back to 1924. That's impossible."

"Good," Levi encouraged. "Keep that in mind."

"And I think you're right about Hecate," he confessed. "She honed in on my weakness and exploited it." Frankie rubbed his head. "She's still trying to. I mean, I see Marie *right there*." He nodded toward a spot a few feet away, but Levi saw nothing.

"Hecate's messing with your head."

Frankie nodded. "And I need you to keep me focused. Her influence is waning, but it's still there."

"So what do we do now?"

"We need more information."

"Okay." Levi looked to his friend. "Where do we get that?"

CHAPTER 19

- SATURDAY, OCTOBER 13, 1984 -

Eddie slept in late Saturday morning. That was the one—and perhaps only—perk of not having the family that he had envisioned. There was no one to interfere with his sleep.

Or maybe it was that he had no one to get up for.

Shuffling into the kitchen, he started the coffee and then went out to get the newspaper from the front porch. The first thing that struck him when he opened the door was the chill. He let out a heavy breath and, sure enough, he could see the air leaving his mouth.

Padding out a few steps, he bent over to grab the paper. Even with his bare feet freezing on the wood, he paused to look down at the bottom porch step he had replaced.

LURED BY MAGIC

Shaking his head, he returned to the warmth of the house and closed the door behind him. He fixed his coffee, then sat down at the kitchen table to read the paper.

The note he had found under the floorboard sat on the table. Eddie was so disgusted with himself for even entertaining the idea that the note had any truth to it that he set his coffee cup over it to block it from his view.

How could I be so gullible? he thought to himself. *I wasted all of that money buying junk from the Apothecary. Am I really that desperate for something to do?*

That was a slippery slope he had no intention on embarking down, so he unfolded the newspaper and started reading.

None of it was particularly interesting. He pulled out the numerous ads and flyers and set them aside, then opened the paper to the next page. He absently reached for his mug and took a sip before setting it back on the note.

As he scanned the inside headlines, one caught his eye: POLICE STILL SEARCHING FOR MISSING MAN. In the lead paragraph, the name was none other than Frankie Walker.

Eddie blinked and held the paper closer to his face to make sure he was reading it correctly. Frankie Walker, the man who sold him his house and—possibly—left him the note under his porch, was missing. He skimmed the rest of the article and saw that he had been missing for over a month.

He sat back in his chair and rubbed the stubble on his chin. "Holy shit." He shook his head and again murmured, "Holy shit."

His mind raced with the interactions over the last couple of days. How evasive the realty office had been. How he had the feeling that Samantha was hiding something. Was it simply shock that Eddie wasn't aware of her father missing? Or did she know more than she was letting on?

His eyes darted to the letter tucked under his coffee mug. Was there any truth to the possibility that Frankie was in 1924?

Eddie shook his head. That was impossible. There was no way that Frankie could've —

But the very same letter that started all of this laid out the details of a spell. A ritual of some sort. If Frankie disappeared without a trace and his own kids were lying to cover for him, maybe Frankie somehow had time traveled.

Eddie shot to his feet and paced around the kitchen with his hands on his head.

This is crazy. Time travel? It's not possible. Then again, neither is witchcraft. But then, the letter says...

Lured by Magic

He dove for the table to retrieve the letter, now stained with coffee. His mug spilled over in his haste, blackening the newspaper in the process, and further spreading to the edges of the table. Eddie didn't pay it any mind. He was too focused on the letter, rereading it again and again.

Frankie Walker, what the hell happened to you?

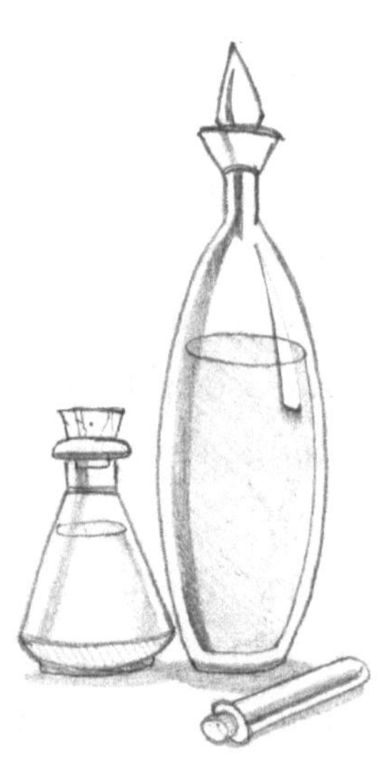

CHAPTER 20

Evelyn woke up on the couch at Tommy's house. It wasn't a restful sleep. In fact, even though a dim, diluted sun shone through the window, she felt just as exhausted as she had when she had decided to try to get some sleep.

At least that much was going for her. In this alternate plane, at least she could actually sleep. If she had shared Tommy's consciousness, all she'd be doing was simply a deep-dive into his psyche while he slept. Either that, or she'd get kicked out of his mind altogether.

Psychic connection was often unpredictable.

She sat up and looked around at the dank and

depressing house. There were still remnants of a once-happy family. Photos around told stories of the past: a mother and a father. A happy and joyful Tommy as a child. The wall contained a growth chart for him at each birthday, with dates and measurements penciled on plaster.

It was sad to see how far a family could deteriorate over time. Worse was the fact that until the psychic connection, Evelyn had no idea that this was the life that Tommy lived. She made a vow to herself that if she ever got out of this that she was going to pay more attention to the people around her.

The bedroom door opened and Tommy shuffled out. His hair was matted in places and standing up in others. He wore wrinkled pajamas that seemed frayed at the seams. He disappeared into the bathroom, and only the faintest sign of the phantom trailed behind him.

Even without Hecate's magic, this is a terrible existence, she thought to herself. *All alone. No family. No friends.* Evelyn wished that she could let him know that she was there somehow. If, for no other reason, than to let him know that he wasn't alone.

After Tommy emerged from the bathroom, he went into the kitchen and fixed himself some toast. There was a sluggishness about him that struck Evelyn as more than just early-morning grogginess. It was as if his very spirit was slowly dying. His will to live was withering away.

In fact, Evelyn felt the same hopelessness in herself. She did her best to fight off the unwanted thoughts, but still they persisted. She feared that the longer she spent in this alternate plane—subjected to the phantom tormenting Tommy and being helpless to do anything about it—that she would lose herself as well. And, as more time passed, that's exactly how she felt.

CHAPTER 21

The next morning, Frankie and Levi sat in the living room of Anna's house and flipped through *The Art of Magic* on the counter. Anna walked in from the kitchen with a large wooden tray. Levi jumped to his feet to assist her.

"Here, let me take that for you." He took the tray from her and stepped aside to allow her room to reach her chair.

"Thank you." She held her large belly as she sank down into the chair.

Levi set the tray with the full assortment of tea preparation on the coffee table next to the magic book.

"Are you sure you should be up on your feet?" Frankie asked.

She sighed. "The doctor told me to take it easy for the rest of my pregnancy. Luckily, that's only a few more weeks."

"How are you feeling?" Levi asked.

"Tired," she said pointedly. "But I'll survive. You said you two were looking for a god?"

Frankie nodded and turned his attention back to *The Art of Magic*. "Technically, she's the Goddess of the Underworld. But lately she's been doing crossroads deals in an effort to maintain her power. After the Greeks and Romans stopped worshipping her, she lost a lot of her power."

Anna nodded. "Hecate?"

Frankie turned to her. "You know her?"

"Only a little," she said. "I think there's a section on her somewhere in there."

"Found it," he said.

Anna smiled. "Just as I thought."

"Looks like she uses phantoms to terrify the living to the point where they feel that trading in their souls is a better option to reality." Levi looked up at Frankie.

"Okay, so I guess you were right," Frankie conceded. "But what do we do about it?"

"You're seeing phantoms?" Anna's eyes darted between the two men, concern evident in her voice.

"Yeah," Levi said. "His late wife."

Frankie rolled his eyes. "Only sometimes. And today I've only seen her twice."

"You were a sobbing mess yesterday, ready to trade in your soul if I hadn't stopped you," Levi said.

"I wasn't going to go through with it."

Levi raised his eyebrows in disbelief. "That's not the impression I got."

"Regardless," Anna cut in. "I don't believe that Hecate's intention is to get you to trade in your soul. She would, of course, accept that. However, I think her main objective with your phantom is simply to create a distraction."

"A distraction from what?" Levi asked.

"Whatever else she's doing," Anna said.

"Like what?" Frankie asked.

"She must have another victim in mind."

"Well," Levi started, "we still never figured out where Evelyn went."

"Just because we haven't seen her, doesn't mean she's missing," Frankie said.

"I'd rather overreact than not do anything and lose her forever."

Frankie nodded. He agreed, but his pride was standing in his way of conceding to that. If he hadn't been influenced by the phantom, then they wouldn't have lost a day in their search to find Evelyn.

LURED BY MAGIC

"She's never missed a day of work," Levi went on. "*And* she was trying to look into Hecate while we were digging up the ritual box at the crossroads. That can't be a coincidence."

"And you still haven't heard from her?" Anna asked.

Frankie shook his head. "No."

"Surely, she would've reported her findings to you, whether she was successful or not."

"That's exactly what I'm saying!" Levi said.

"So what do we do?" Frankie asked.

Anna thought for a moment. "You stop Hecate, and then you find Evelyn."

"And what if Hecate is the one who has her?" Levi asked.

"Then you'll discover that when you stop the evil goddess."

CHAPTER 22

"You're late!" Eugene shouted at Tommy when he walked into Meyer's Place. Eugene was the manager of the restaurant when Levi wasn't there.

"S-Sorry." Tommy's eyes scanned the ground, the kitchen, his fingers—anywhere but Eugene's face.

"If I wasn't short-staffed, you'd be fired," he said. "I need someone reliable."

"I stay late—"

"You wouldn't have to if you showed up on time," Eugene said.

From the alternate plane, Evelyn felt an almost physical blow from each verbal attack that was thrown at Tommy. The psychic connection seemed to be growing stronger and she worried that if she didn't find a way to separate herself from him, they'd eventually be tied together forever.

Eugene put his hands on his hips and huffed. "I don't have time to sit here and lecture you anymore. We've got a rush coming. Get to work, or your ass is on the street. Got that?"

Tommy nodded, then stepped toward the hook to grab his apron from the wall.

"And *don't* be late again!" Eugene added.

While Evelyn felt a blow from the verbal assault, the feelings passed by the time Tommy got to work. In fact, *all* of her feelings seemed to pass. There was no sense of hope or despair or excitement or anything. It was as if she were numb. Completely apathetic to everything.

Is this what Tommy's feeling? she wondered. If the two were psychically connected, then it made sense that she would be picking up on his emotions as well. She had definitely been picking up on his sense of hopelessness since she had first arrived on the plane. But this was a different level altogether. This was the absence of any kind of feeling, which scared her more than if he had been feeling *something*.

It was like Tommy had given up.

And the scariest part of all was that if Tommy had given up, it wouldn't be long before Evelyn felt the same. She needed to get back to her own consciousness. And soon.

"Take Table Four," Eugene told Tommy. "We'll work you into the rotation. Johnny is going to need his break soon."

Evelyn followed Tommy as he grabbed a large tray, propped it against his hip, and stacked the plates onto the tray to carry out into the dining room.

If she was going to send a message to someone—to try to get help to get out of this plane—then she needed to actually be around people. Holing up in the kitchen was not going to help any.

So when Tommy carried the food out into the dining room, she happily followed. To her surprise, the front door opened and Frankie and Levi came rushing in. They didn't run, but the look of determination on their faces and their fast paces said that they were focused. On a mission.

"Hey!" Evelyn called to them. "Frankie! Levi! Stop! I need help! It's Evelyn!"

Her words fell flat. Neither one of them seemed to notice her at all. They just continued to the back of the restaurant and up the stairs toward the hotel rooms. It was as if her words were lost in the ether. And perhaps

LURED BY MAGIC

they were. The thought of it made her feel even more alone.

Maybe she wasn't ever going to get her life back.

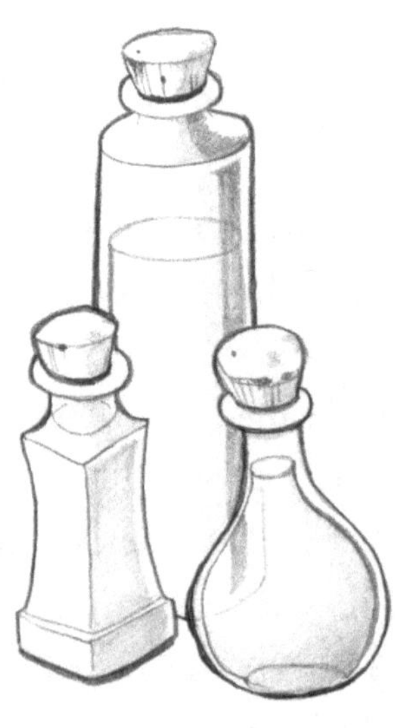

CHAPTER 23

Frankie and Levi sat on the floor in Frankie's hotel room. There was a basin of water sitting between the two of them with four yellow candles around it, placed in the directions of north, south, east, and west.

"You sure you're okay to do this?" Levi asked.

Frankie breathed in a deep breath. "I'll give it a shot." Over Levi's shoulder, he saw Marie again. He blinked, but her image persisted.

It's not real, he told himself. But it was easier said than done when he *wished* his wife was actually there. That was impossible, though. And he had to focus.

Holding his hands above the water basin, he recited:

I call on the strength of my power.
Show Evelyn's face in the water.

The two of them looked at the bowl, which sat undisturbed on the floor.

"Was that it?" Levi asked.

Frankie let out a frustrated sigh. "No. The water is supposed to show where she is in the reflection."

Levi peered into the bowl again, then looked up at the witch. "I don't see anything."

He glared at him. "That's because it didn't work."

"Try again."

Frankie tried again, with the same results. After the second attempt, he slumped backward onto the floor and rubbed his hands over his face.

"What's going on?" Levi asked. "Is it the phantom? Is she bothering you again?"

"It's not the phantom." Frankie sat up. "At least, not in a direct way. It's just that—she's *right there*!" He pointed behind Levi, who turned to look over his shoulder, then turned back to his friend.

"There's no one there."

"Well, there is for me."

"So ignore her."

"Easier said than done."

Levi nodded an acknowledgement, then changed

118

tacts. "What about trying to focus, instead, on Evelyn? Just close your eyes, think about her—try to connect with her on a more spiritual level—and then cast the spell."

Frankie raised his eyebrows and smirked. "I never thought I'd see the day when the nonmagical gave advice in spellcasting to a witch."

"Maybe if you weren't whining so much you could do it yourself."

The witch shot his friend a look, but then closed his eyes and took the advice. He initially saw Marie in his mind, even when his eyes were closed. After a few seconds, he was able to push that aside and focus only on Evelyn. On who she truly was as a person. To try to connect to her spirit. Her soul.

When he felt prepared, he held his hands out over the basin again, careful to keep his eyes shut and his mind trained on Evelyn. For the third time, he recited the spell:

I call on the strength of my power.
Show Evelyn's face in the water.

"It's working!" Levi's voice broke into Frankie's concentration.

The witch's eyes fluttered open and he looked into the basin with his friend.

Lured by Magic

"Is that…?" Frankie asked.

"That's…downstairs," Levi confirmed. "The dining room. Actually, is that in real time?"

"It should be."

They exchanged looks.

"She's downstairs?" Levi asked.

Frankie didn't answer, but shot to his feet and raced out the door. His feet carried him down the steps so fast that he was afraid he might tumble the rest of the way down.

On the first floor, with Levi hot on his heels, Frankie burst into the dining room and stopped.

There was nothing out of the ordinary from what they could tell. The diners were enjoying their meals, only looking up at the urgency—and noisiness—of Frankie and Levi. And yet not a single one of them was Evelyn.

"It didn't work?" Levi asked.

"But it did!" Frankie scanned the faces again and again, searching for his friend.

"Maybe…maybe the phantom has a stronger effect on you than you thought?" Levi suggested.

Frankie shook his head. "No. I think something else is going on."

"Like what?"

The witch sighed. "I wish I knew."

CHAPTER 24

Evelyn watched as Frankie and Levi rushed into the dining room. The two of them looked around, scanning the faces of the people in the crowd.

They're figuring it out, she thought to herself. *They're looking for me. They're trying to rescue me!*

It was the biggest rush of emotion that she had felt since she had arrived on the alternate plane, and yet it was still subdued. Like the emotion was hidden behind a veil. Detectable, but not fully present.

Frankie's shoulders slumped and Levi stepped in closer to him. They talked quietly and Evelyn couldn't make out what they were saying.

She took a step forward, but was met with the

invisible forcefield that kept her in close proximity to Tommy, who was taking the order of a table at the front of the restaurant. She continued to push, half-wondering if maybe that was the answer for getting out of this mess: just breaking the barrier that had been placed on her.

The forcefield pushed back and she stumbled to the floor. When she scrambled back to her feet, Tommy had moved closer. She could finally make out what her friends were saying.

"…this is what I saw," Frankie told Levi. "You saw it too, didn't you? You saw Evelyn right here."

Her heart burst with excitement. They *were* looking for her!

"Well, something went wrong," Levi said. "What do you think it was?"

Evelyn couldn't hear Frankie's response. She scooted backwards by the edge of the forcefield as Tommy disappeared back into the kitchen.

She had made it to her feet when Tommy returned to the dining room. At this point, however, Frankie and Levi had taken a few steps toward the door. Frankie still kept looking into the dining room, scanning faces.

"Wait!" Evelyn called, knowing it was no use. "Frankie! Listen to me!"

She was pulled back again as Tommy went to the bar to fill out a receipt. She studied him.

I have to get out of here, she thought. *I have to find a way to send a message to Frankie and Levi. Let them know that I* am *here. There's obviously a way. They saw me somehow, through whatever spell Frankie had cast.*

Then she got an idea. She was connected to Tommy psychically. If she touched his physical body too, and focused on taking control of his body for only a second, maybe she could use Tommy's voice to tell Frankie and Levi that she was there and needed help.

It was a long shot. She had never done that kind of magic before, but she couldn't just let the opportunity pass by without doing *something*.

Reaching out, she placed a hand on Tommy's shoulder. Instantly, her vision went black and her consciousness was bombarded with Tommy's phantom shrieking at her as terrible scenes from Tommy's life flashed through her mind like a projector screen.

Tommy shivering at night in his room.

Tommy's feet, sore and calloused from long-worn shoes.

Tommy's mother dying.

Tommy going to work and being scolded for not making enough money.

Tommy sitting alone in his house.

Tommy's father dying.

The loneliness.

LURED BY MAGIC

The despair.

The will to live, slowly dwindling away.

The flashes passed by her so quickly that she couldn't focus on any particular one for any length of time. Still, she felt the terrible feeling of emptiness after the images blissfully ceased.

Evelyn crumpled to the ground, feeling weakened and drained. The longer she stayed in this alternate plane, the more debilitated she became. And yet, as she watched Frankie and Levi disappear into the kitchen, she realized that she had no hope of ever getting out alive.

CHAPTER 25

Frankie wasn't convinced that his spell had gone wrong. Sure, he had been affected by the phantom—which still lingered close by him—but the spell had gone just the way it was meant to. It had found Evelyn and showed her in the water. The fact that they couldn't see her when they went down to the restaurant to find her simply meant that something else was at play.

Likely something paranormal.

Something like Hecate.

Frankie and Levi stepped into the kitchen, where they found Levi's restaurant manager working at the grill.

"Hey, Eugene," Levi called to him when they walked in. The food on the grill was sizzling, sending plumes of smoke up into the air. Elsewhere, dishes clanged and banged as everyone worked diligently in their own private corners.

The middle-aged man with the large belly and grease stains all over his T-shirt turned to Levi and held a hand to his ear. "Huh?" he grunted loudly.

"We wanted to talk to you," Levi told him.

Eugene shook his head and shouted back, "Can't talk right now. I'm too busy."

Levi shot him a look. "The crowd is winding down. You can pass the buck for five minutes while I ask you something."

The gruff man rolled his eyes, then turned down the heat on the grill, and the sizzling of the pan quieted. "What is it?"

Levi turned to Frankie to take the lead in the questioning.

"Well—" Frankie started.

"Speak up," Eugene said. "I can't hear you."

The witch cleared his voice and tried again. Louder this time. "We were wondering if you've noticed anything weird lately."

"Weird how?" Eugene kept his attention on the grill as he flipped the patty he was cooking.

"It could be anything out of the ordinary," Frankie explained. "Have you seen anything that's different from how it usually is?"

Eugene shook his head. "Not really. Why you asking about everyone else's business?"

Frankie sidestepped that question by asking his own question. "What about your employees? Has anyone been acting off lately? Out of character?"

He chuckled and pushed around the burger on the skillet. "Haven't noticed much. Then again, I try not to socialize with my employees too much. I pay them to work for me, not talk to me."

"Oh," Frankie said quietly. So much so that he doubted Eugene even heard him.

"Are we done? I really need to get back to things. We're a little behind since Tommy showed up late again."

"Tommy was late again?" Levi chirped up. He exchanged a look with Frankie to indicate that that behavior *was* out of the ordinary.

Eugene nodded. "Twice now. Damn kid is lucky he even still has a job."

"Anything else that's been strange about him?" Levi asked.

The manager shrugged. "Can't say I've noticed. He's been quieter than usual, I guess. But I'd be too if my boss reamed me out and I knew I was in the wrong. Like I said, he's lucky he's even still here."

"Is he usually quiet?" Frankie asked Levi.

He nodded. "Pretty much. But by the end of his shift he usually opens up." He pointed to indicate which one they were talking about.

Frankie had been helping out with Levi at the restaurant, but he was still a long way off from knowing everybody's names and their temperaments. Especially with all of the magical crises that they needed to fix since he had started working at Meyer's Place.

"You don't think he's tied to anything, do you?" Levi asked.

Frankie didn't respond. He watched Tommy come in and take an order. When Tommy disappeared back into the dining room with a tray of food, Frankie deliberated for only a few seconds before pushing through the doors into the dining room himself.

As his eyes scanned the room for where Tommy had gone, something else caught his eye. Or rather, some*one*. Entering the dining room with an arrogant smile on her face was none other than the fallen goddess Hecate.

CHAPTER 26

By the time Evelyn had regained her strength enough to pull herself up from the floor, Frankie and Levi were emerging from the kitchen again. She watched as their eyes locked on someone across the room.

Hecate.

Evelyn whipped her eyes back toward Frankie and saw his jaw clench in anger. Yet nobody made a move in such a public place. Perhaps that was the reason Hecate decided to surface here instead of elsewhere, like the crossroads. Then again, no matter where Hecate went, she was typically the one in control.

An idea struck Evelyn. If Hecate was the Goddess of

the Underworld, and gatekeeper to the crossroads, then hypothetically she could exist in two places at once — maybe even two *planes* at once.

Evelyn looked over at the disgraced goddess for any trace of acknowledgment on her part. However, if Evelyn's theory was true, Hecate had probably developed a way to focus on whatever plane she wanted to by shutting out the other noise. Meaning, she wouldn't see Evelyn until Evelyn gave her a reason to look.

"Hecate!" Evelyn barked suddenly. Her voice was muted. Like trying to scream in a dream.

But it did the trick.

Suddenly, Hecate's eyes moved away from Frankie and Levi, and she stopped in her slow pursuit of them. She looked around in Evelyn's direction, as if the oracle were lost in a crowded room or something.

She must be searching through all the places she simultaneously exists in, Evelyn thought.

Finally, Hecate's eyes locked on Evelyn and she sneered.

The goddess turned on the oracle with venom in her eyes.

This is it, Evelyn thought. *Say something. Do something. What's the plan?*

Before she could come up with one, Hecate caught the attention of Frankie and Levi slowly sneaking out through the back room.

Hecate clenched her fists as she watched them leave, then turned to Evelyn. "We'll finish this later."

Evelyn was too stunned to do anything.

Hecate disappeared through the back room as well. Only then did Evelyn have the idea to follow her, but she came up short when she hit the invisible forcefield that kept her tied to Tommy's proximity.

She glanced back at him and saw that he was making change at the register behind the bar, completely oblivious to the exchange that had happened on multiple planes at once, right in front of his eyes.

She rolled her eyes. *The nonmagical are so oblivious sometimes.*

CHAPTER 27

In the back alley, Frankie and Levi waited for Hecate. The sun had begun to set and the two stood in the shadows behind the buildings lining State Street.

Hecate emerged only a moment after they had. Frankie was glad that they were able to draw her out, away from the crowd of innocent bystanders in the restaurant. The last thing Meyer's Place needed was another brawl that would likely permanently shut the place down.

"Well," she said. "It looks like we've finally reached a point where we can have a conversation."

"What do you want?" Frankie demanded.

She raised her eyebrows. "Easy now. I believe I'm the only one in a position to be so *aggressive*."

"You took our friend. We want her back."

Hecate laughed. "Oh, trust me. I had nothing to do with what happened to your friend. If I had, then she'd be somewhere *so much* worse than where she is now."

Frankie and Levi exchanged glances.

"But you do know where she is?" Levi asked.

"Of course. I'm the gatekeeper of the worlds."

"Then where is she?" Frankie asked.

She shook her head. "You're wasting your time on her. That's not why I'm here."

"I don't give a damn why you're here," Frankie spat. "Unless you tell us where our friend is, then you can save whatever it is you came here to tell us."

"Oh, is that so?" she asked. "So you wouldn't be interested in making a deal?"

"No," the witch answered easily.

"Really? Not even to return you to your own time?"

Frankie opened his mouth to reply, but stopped short. After a pause, he asked, "How?"

"Ah," she said with a chuckle. "Now I've caught your interest."

"Just tell us what you're suggesting so we can rest assured we made the right choice when we turn you down," Levi said.

Hecate shot a murderous glance his way. "I'm not here for you, *mortal*. You can just go somewhere else." She raised her hand to flick him away, but Frankie was faster. He used his own power to knock her hand back.

"Don't you touch him," he warned. "Just tell us what you want to tell us."

She sighed. "Oh, all right. You aren't making this nearly as fun as I thought it'd be. I would like to propose a deal: I'll summon Zanabar back to 1924 and negotiate an arrangement that will send you back to your time."

"In exchange for what?" Levi asked.

She rolled her eyes. "Oh, would you shut up!"

"You want my soul," Frankie finished.

"Well, yes."

Levi looked between Frankie and Hecate, then asked the goddess, "Why do you think he'd agree to that?"

"Because it's the only way to get him to return back to his time, *and* it would ensure that no one else here is bothered by me again." She rolled her eyes again, miming boredom. "You see, I'd collect your soul in exchange for Tommy's."

Frankie wasn't surprised that she was hunting him. Not after what Eugene had just told them about Tommy's strange behavior as of late.

Lured by Magic

"Forget it," Levi said. "If Frankie doesn't have a soul, then there's no point in him going back to his own time."

Hecate let out an annoyed sigh. "This isn't up to you to decide." She turned to Frankie. "I was asking him."

The witch thought it over. It was very similar to the idea that he had had himself. Only, in this proposal, Tommy—and everyone else in Erie in 1924—would be safe. Sacrifice one to save many more? It seemed like it was a fair trade.

"Frankie…" Levi muttered, turning to his friend. "You can't seriously be considering this. Remember everything we talked about."

Frankie wouldn't meet his friend's eyes. He studied the ground. "I know. But…"

"I see you're having a hard time deciding," Hecate cut in. "So to show that I'm being sincere, allow me to summon Zanabar here as a way to flex my power."

"No, wait!" Levi called to her, but it was too late.

Hecate swung her arms out, the skeleton keys in one hand rattling, while she pointed the torch in the other hand toward the ground. The flame from the torch erupted from the top and covered a giant area on the ground.

Frankie and Levi both jumped back, feeling the heat of the flame flick against their skin.

From the flames rose the manipulative sorcerer Zanabar. He roared in dissatisfaction at being summoned.

"What is the meaning of this?" he demanded, turning on Hecate.

She gestured toward Frankie. "I heard that you have some unfinished business and I may be interested in negotiating a trade with you."

The sorcerer turned to the witch and snarled. "Ah. The betrayer."

Levi took another step back.

"You weren't honest about the terms of the deal from the beginning." Frankie held up his hand, ready to use his magic if he needed. Truthfully, though, Zanabar very likely would've overpowered anything that Frankie could throw at him. The only hope was that Zanabar was somehow weakened and disoriented from the jump through time.

The sorcerer took steady steps toward them. "Thanks to you, I lost out on the genie half-breed *and* I was expelled from 1924."

"And thanks to *you*, I was tricked into coming to 1924 and then left here as if my life in 1984 didn't even matter," Frankie countered.

Zanabar brought his hands out from under his robe and started muttering incantations in another language.

LURED BY MAGIC

"What is he doing?" Levi panicked.

"Doesn't matter. Just run!"

Levi led Frankie down the far side of the alley. Behind them, Zanabar's magic took hold, sending an earth-shaking blast in their direction and knocking them to the ground.

Frankie spun around just as Zanabar was descending on Levi.

"Maybe I could kill your powerless friend here as restitution for your betrayal." Zanabar extended his hand to grab at Levi's shirt.

"Ah!" Levi shouted as he was pulled back by the sorcerer, who held an arm around his throat and pressed him close to his body, like a shield.

"Now's your chance," Zanabar said. "It's you or him. What's it going to be?"

Frankie looked around for something to use his magic on and his eyes landed on the bottom rung of a fire escape ladder. Aiming his hand up, he focused his energy on ripping the pipe off the ladder and toward the sorcerer.

It made a direct hit, slamming hard against Zanabar's head. The impact caused him to collapse to the ground, right on top of Levi. Frankie rushed up and helped his friend get out from under Zanabar's weight.

"You okay?" Frankie asked Levi.

He nodded. They both looked back toward the back entrance of the restaurant where Hecate stood, watching the encounter with her arms crossed and a smirk on her face.

"Let's get out of here before she can do anything else," Levi said.

"Good idea."

CHAPTER 28

"I know we don't have very many options to turn to here," Levi said as he and Frankie walked along Arlington Road, "but don't you think it's a little risky to take refuge at your pregnant grandmother's house?"

Frankie shook his head as they turned down the sidewalk leading up to Anna's house from the street. "I don't like it, either, but like you said, we don't have a lot of options. And we need another witch to help us figure this out. I'm not at full strength and you don't have any magic, so if we're going to find Evelyn and stop Hecate, then we need to take some risks."

Levi shrugged. "If you say so."

Lured by Magic

At the door, Frankie knocked and waited for Anna to answer.

Only, when the door swung open it was a young man standing on the other side. He appeared to be about the same age as Levi, only a few years older than Frankie's own daughters. He had sandy blond hair and he wore a blue collared shirt and jeans.

It took a measured level of effort for Frankie not to blurt out his grandfather's name.

"Can I help you?" William asked.

Frankie stared. His mind was too caught up in seeing his grandfather as a young man that he couldn't bring himself to say anything.

Beside him, Levi cleared his throat and asked, "We—uh—we were hoping to talk to Anna. Is she home?"

William kept his eyes on Frankie. "I'm sorry, but have we met? You look familiar."

Frankie stared into his grandfather's eyes as visions of the past floated to his memory: driving around town in William's worn pickup truck, likely on the way to get a tool or a part from the hardware store to work on something in the house; William holding both of Frankie's daughters the day each of them were born; the funeral, where Frankie mourned the life of the man who now stood before him in his youth.

"No, you haven't," Levi cut in. "This is Frankie and I'm Levi. We're—"

"They're witches," Anna's voice said from behind William. She appeared in the doorway next to him. "At least, Frankie is. They're friends of mine."

William looked down and studied his wife. She smiled and nodded. "It's okay, dear."

With that, William stepped aside to allow them to enter.

Frankie and Levi walked into the house, suddenly feeling like strangers.

"Why doesn't everyone sit down?" William suggested. "Would you like something to drink? Tea? I'd love to get to know some of my wife's friends. Especially if there's another witch in town."

Frankie offered a tight smile. "That would be nice, thanks."

When Anna turned to the kitchen, William grabbed her arm. "I'll get it all together, honey. You shouldn't be on your feet."

Anna rolled her eyes, but smiled at her husband. She led Frankie and Levi into the living room while William disappeared into the kitchen.

"Sorry," Frankie murmured quietly when they were alone. "I didn't know he'd be home."

Anna adjusted her position in her seat, unable to find

a comfortable spot. "It's all right. It was bound to happen sooner than later anyway. I would just like to keep your identity a secret. He's to never know that you're our…grandson?"

Frankie nodded.

She raised her eyebrows and shook her head. "That's still something I just can't get used to. Anyway, it's better if fewer people know about who you are. Normally, William would've been working, but since the doctor told me I should take it easy, he's been home more often than usual in order to take care of me." She glanced back toward the kitchen. "It's sweet, the way he dotes on me, but I'll be glad when he goes back to work too."

Frankie laughed. He knew exactly what she was talking about. As much as he loved Marie, he remembered the days when he just needed time to himself. Now, of course, he craved any opportunity to see his wife. Even when the visions he had of her weren't really her at all.

"Well," Anna said, "I assume there's a reason for your late visit?"

"We're in a bit of a bind," Levi started, but stopped short when William came in with a tray of tea and teacups.

He set it down on the coffee table, closest to Anna.

"Oh, why thank you, dear," Anna said. "This looks great."

William began to sit in the chair beside his wife, but waved her hand in his direction.

"Uh, honey. Shouldn't you be working on that piece for the Marbles' new house?" Anna leaned forward and began fixing her tea. "And did you ever finish the baby's crib and rocker?"

Her husband nodded. "No, I haven't. Excuse me, gentlemen. I have a lot of work to do. I suppose we'll have to get to know each other another time." He leaned in close to Anna and kissed her cheek. "I'll be right outside if you need anything."

She patted her husband's cheek. "I'll be fine, dear. Thank you."

They waited until the back door closed before they resumed talking.

Anna brought her cup to her lips and took a small sip. "So, you're in a bind?"

With that, Frankie and Levi recounted their story.

Chapter 29

- Sunday, October 14, 1984 -

The congregation stood at the end of Sunday mass and began filing down the center aisle to the back of the church. Eddie waited in the last pew until everyone had cleared out, then approached the altar.

He knelt to one knee and made the sign of the cross before stepping onto the altar.

"Father Thompson," he called to the priest.

Father Thompson had just ducked into the sacristy, but popped his head back out at the call of his name. "Oh, hello. Do you need something?"

Eddie looked around. He felt very out of place standing on the altar of the church that he had stopped attending a long time ago. Although, having been raised

Catholic, his faith had never truly left him. It was as if it had been finely ingrained into his very being.

Perhaps that was why he was having such a hard time.

"Well," he said, "I was hoping to talk to you."

Father Thompson looked back into the sacristy with hesitation. "Truthfully, I have the next mass to prepare for."

"Oh. Okay then. That's fine. It's okay. I can—I can come back some other time then."

The priest's face softened. "Can you give me five minutes to change out of my vestments? I could spare ten minutes for you."

Eddie smiled. "Of course. I'll wait right here. Thank you." He made his way down the altar and sat in the front pew.

While he waited, he couldn't help but take in the spectacle that was the religious altar in front of him. He thought of everything it stood for. The strength, the guidance, and the sense of community. How did the note that Frankie left him meld with what he had always believed to be true? Was it possible that the supernatural existed? Then again, wasn't the belief in God and the miracles He performed a belief in something superiorly natural as well? Wasn't that exactly what the supernatural was?

"Okay," Father Thompson said in a cheerful voice. "Would you like to go to the confessional?"

Eddie shook his head. "No, we can talk out here, if that's okay with you." He slid over to allow the priest to sit.

The old man took his seat with a slight grown. "I'm not as young as I used to be," he joked. "What's on your mind?"

"What's the church's view on witchcraft?" The question had sounded subtler in his mind, but out loud it was as jarring as shattering glass.

Father Thompson's eyes widened and he took in a deep breath. "Well…this may be controversial in my profession, given the rise in satanic worshippers across the country, but I think when it comes to witchcraft, it's perfectly okay to enjoy as entertainment, as long as it's understood that it's fictional. When it comes to believing in someone for guidance, or relying on the teachings of someone, there really is only one true God." He pointed upward to drive his point home.

Eddie nodded thoughtfully. "Of course."

"*Are* you talking about satanic worship?"

"No. Not at all," Eddie responded quickly. "No, it's just…" He trailed off, wondering how exactly to tell the story. Or rather, how much to tell. "Honestly, I found this letter under my porch. I didn't think much of it, but it's written by someone I know—or knew. In the letter, he asks me to cast a spell."

Father Thompson sat back, taking in Eddie's story without a word.

"It seemed fairly harmless at first, so I went to this, um…occult shop." He cringed and glanced over.

"It's okay," the priest said with a smile. "We're all curious."

"Anyway, the guy at the shop seemed to think that the spell was pretty simple. It's not like it asked for me to sacrifice a lamb or anything." His attempt at a joke fell flat and when he noticed he was the only one laughing, he quickly continued. "Anyway, I thought it the whole thing was a joke—especially because the letter was dated 1924 or something. But then I saw in the newspaper that my friend has been missing for a while. The same friend who supposedly left me the letter." He shrugged and rubbed his hands together. "And now I'm wondering if he left the letter for me because he needed my help."

Father Thompson let out a breath. "If you believe your friend is in trouble, then it's the police you should be talking to and not me. At least not at first."

"I thought of that. Obviously, I did. But I just can't see how the letter would matter to finding Frankie. Nothing in that letter gives any context as to why the spell needed to be cast or where he is—or was. Or even why he was taken. The police would think it's a joke."

"So then why take it seriously at all?"

Eddie thought about this for a moment. "Because the letter said that it was very important and that he was asking me to do it as a friend."

Father Thompson let out a sigh. "Well, I certainly cannot condone any act that's against the word of God. However, I think what you're really dealing with here isn't so much about witchcraft as much as it is about helping a friend in need, which the church fully supports."

"Yeah. Yeah, I guess that's it. I didn't think of it like that."

"But be careful. As I said, witchcraft is okay as long as everyone understands that it's fictional. Maybe your friend just needs you to believe in him."

Eddie smiled. "You're right. Maybe that's all he needs."

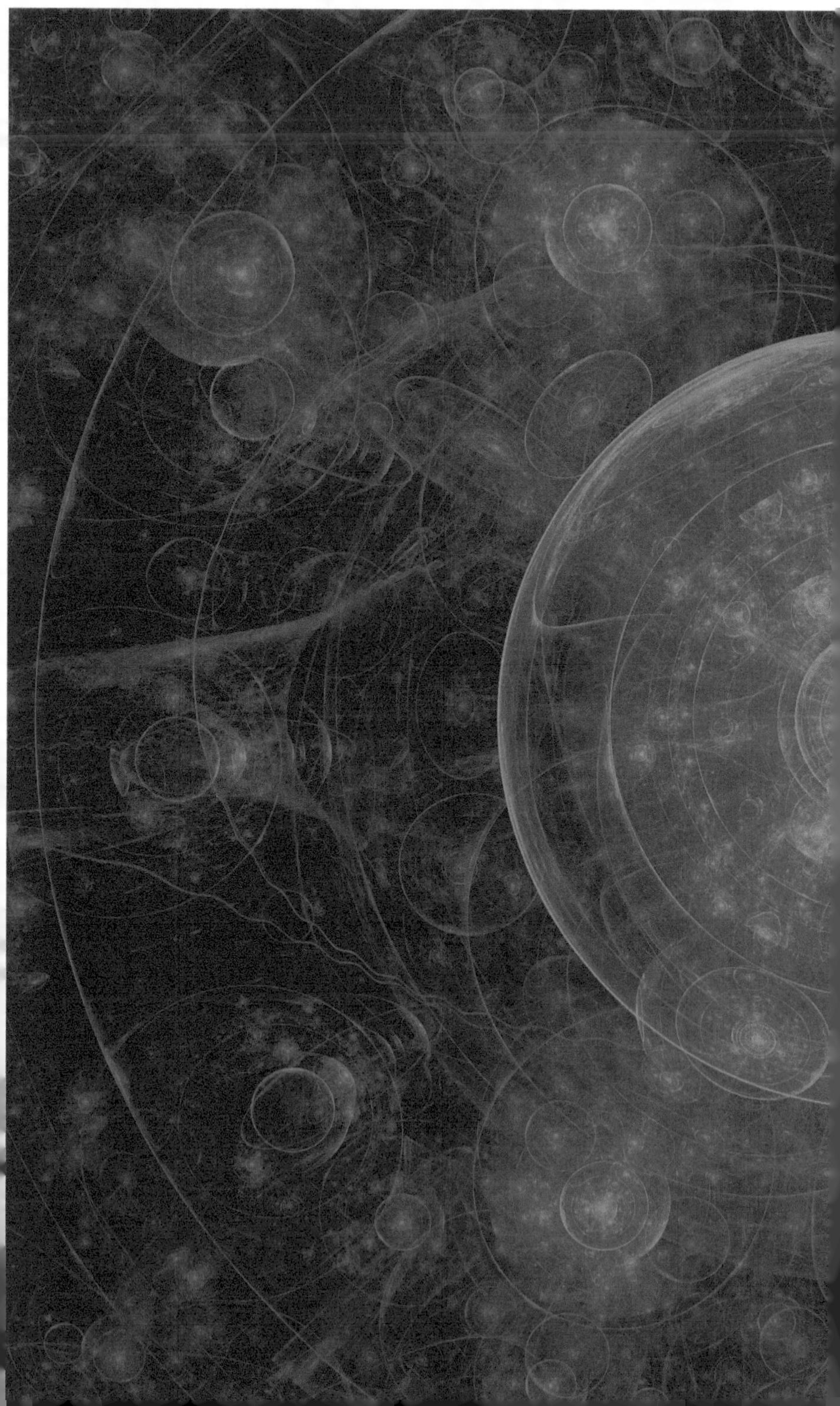

CHAPTER 30

"Okay." Anna sat back in her chair and rubbed her forehead with closed eyes. "To clarify, you're saying that in the time since you were here this morning, you've only gotten in worse trouble with Hecate, you *haven't* found Evelyn, and now there's a sorcerer coming after you as well?"

"Yeah, that pretty much covers it." Levi dropped his eyes to the floor.

"And we don't really know how to go about fixing any of it," Frankie added.

"That much is obvious. You've only dug yourself into a deeper hole since I last talked to you. I can't even let you out of my sight without you running off and making things worse." She released another sigh.

Frankie and Levi both sunk into their respective chairs for being scolded.

"Lucky for the both of you, I think I may have a solution to your problem," she said. "But it's going to take some work."

"What are you thinking?" Frankie asked.

"There's a recipe for a potion that will strip the powers of anyone who is supernaturally inclined," she explained. "It's a very powerful recipe, so it's hidden by magic in my magic book—or, I guess, *our* magic book." She smiled at her grandson.

"I've never heard of such a recipe," Frankie said. "Where in the book is it?"

"Somewhere that the wrong people wouldn't be able to find it." She pointed up the staircase. "Levi, would you be a dear and go up and get the book? It should be on the landing."

Levi jumped to his feet and raced up the stairs.

"I'm surprised you let him go alone," Frankie said.

Anna cradled her belly. "I'm going to have to learn to trust people. After all, I'm about to have a piece of my heart that's walking, talking, breathing. That's going to be a huge leap of faith."

Frankie nodded. He knew exactly what she meant. Letting your kids make their own mistakes, or get hurt by other people, was one of the biggest challenges of parenthood.

"But," she went on, "judging by the way that you turned out, it's obvious that I did something right. If you think Levi is trustworthy, then I have to trust your judgment."

Levi returned a moment later with the large tome held in both of his hands. He handed it to Anna, who struggled to balance it on her lap around her belly.

"So we're making this potion for Zanabar?" Frankie asked. "Convince him to take me back to 1984, then force him to take it?"

Anna rolled her eyes. "No. Your problem with the sorcerer is something that we'll have to figure out later. I'm talking about Hecate. I've been thinking about her all day. This Zanabar fellow is a new issue that I'll have to spend some time thinking about before I bail you out of that one."

Levi smirked. "At least she's honest."

Frankie shot him a look.

Anna ignored them both. "We make the potion, then we get Hecate to drink it, which will make her mortal," she explained. "*Then* you'll have to banish her to the underworld, where she'll be forced to stay permanently because she'll have no power."

Frankie raised his eyebrows in speculation. "And

your potion will be strong enough to remove a god's powers?"

"Ah, but she isn't just any old god, is she? She's a disgraced one. Her lack of followers means that her power has already been considerably weakened. If ever there were a time to strike, it's now."

"So you're saying that she gets her powers from believers, like Santa Claus?" Frankie asked.

Again, this warranted an annoyed look from Anna. "Yes, I suppose if that's the way you want to think about it."

"All I know is that, if this is the way Hecate is when she's weak, then I'd hate to see her at full strength," Levi said.

"Exactly," Anna said. "So the two of you better not go pissing off any other gods. If so, then no amount of witchcraft will be able to help you."

"Okay, but if Hecate is stripped of her powers and banished to the underworld for eternity, what's to say that she can't sweet-talk her way out of it?" Frankie asked. "I mean, she's been the gatekeeper to hell for—well, forever. She's obviously built some connections over the centuries. What's to say that a friend of hers won't help her escape back to our world?"

Anna nodded. "Yes, it's true that she's been in this role for a long time, however, she has denied many people in that time. And burned even more bridges with people. It's very unlikely that she has any friends."

"But it's still possible," Levi wondered.

"Anything's possible," Anna said. "However, I don't think she'll have much time to converse with anyone. Once she's mortal, she'll be tormented in hell for her sins just like every other mortal banished to the underworld."

"There's a lot of question marks in this plan," Frankie pointed.

"And yet it's the best one we've got." Anna turned to a page in the magic book. "Here it is. Let's get started."

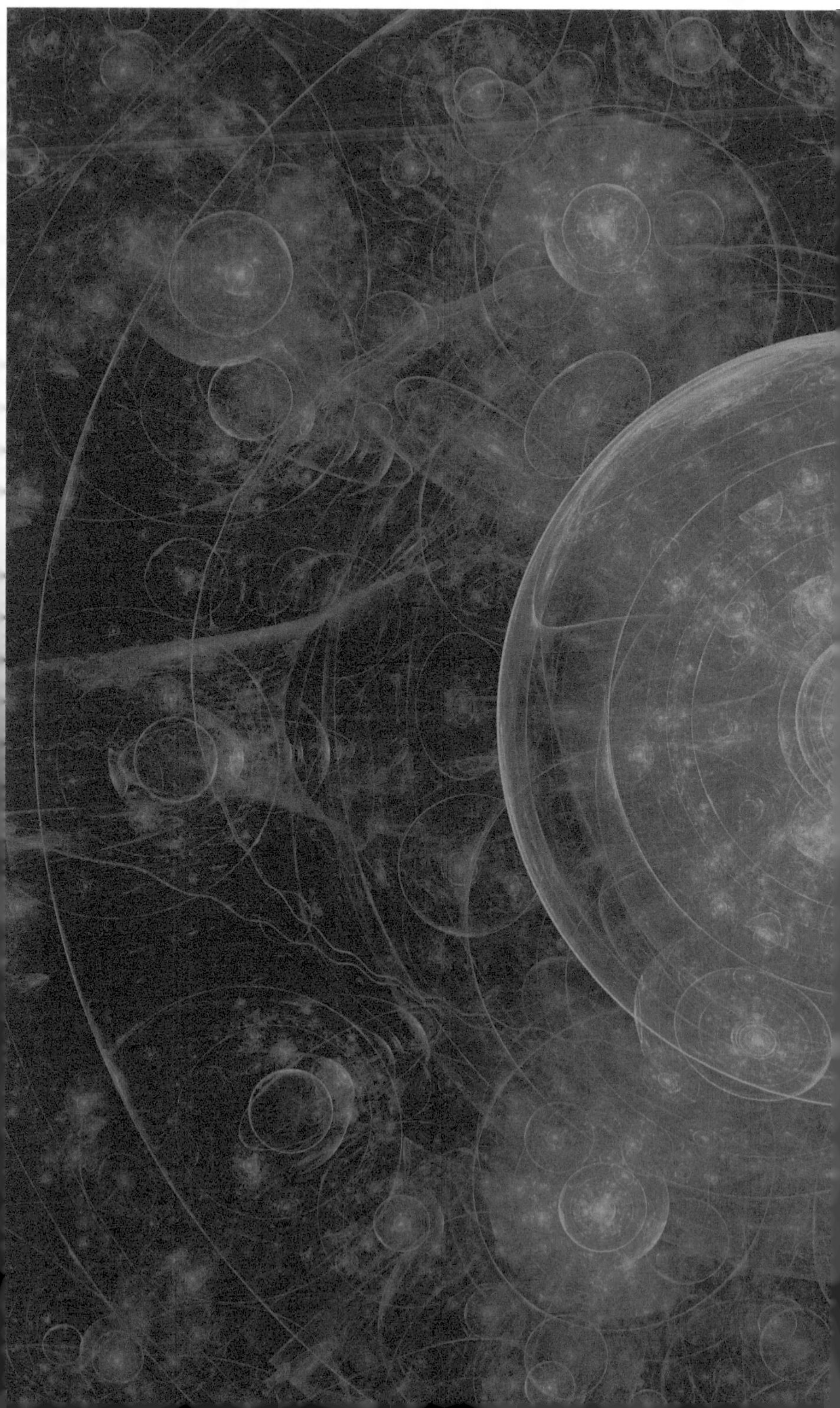

CHAPTER 31

Anna set up Frankie and Levi in their only spare bedroom. William wasn't very happy about the unexpected overnight guests— especially two that he had never met before, and never had the chance to get to know. Frankie wasn't sure exactly what Anna had told him to convince him that it was okay, but he was glad to have a safe place to spend the night.

"I'm sorry that the two of you have to share," she said as she brought an extra set of pillows and blankets into the room and set them on one of the beds. "But we have the other room set up for the baby."

"I'm just glad that we each have our own bed,"

Frankie said. Even though it was a twin-size, it was better than nothing.

"If you need anything, William and I are just next door. Good night." She disappeared into the hall, closing the door behind her.

Levi kicked off his shoes by his bed and climbed under the covers.

Frankie did the same and laid back against the pillows. "Never did I think that I'd be in my forties and having a sleepover at a friend's house."

"Would you consider it a friend's house if it's the house you live in?" Levi asked.

The witch chuckled. "True."

The two of them were quiet as they unwound from the day's events. Frankie studied the shadows on the ceiling, cast there by the lamp sitting on the table between the two beds.

"What room is this?" Levi asked quietly. "In your time?"

"My daughter Samantha's," he said. "The smaller room next door was my other daughter's. Kathy."

"So the one over there is yours?" Levi pointed in the direction of William and Anna's room.

"In 1984," Frankie said. "But actually, at some point or another in my life, I've lived in each of these rooms up here. The small room was mine up until my grandfather moved out."

"William?"

"Yeah."

"Then you moved into this one?" Levi asked.

"Yeah. My family has always had multiple generations living under one roof, so the oldest generation always had the biggest room because they were usually the ones who lived in this house the longest. So after my grandfather moved out, my parents took over that room and I took this one. Then when they left, I took that room and my girls each got their own room. At least, until my parents moved back in. Then they just took this room."

"Oh, I see. That's kind of cool that you've had so many family members living under one room.

"Yeah," Frankie muttered. In truth, he felt like he was breaking a tradition. The multi-generational home ended with him. When he and Marie had first gotten married and were only thinking about kids, he and his parents got into a huge argument about living arrangements. It all was sparked over Frankie's own insecurity that he was not maturing in the way that he had imagined. The way the rest of his friends were.

Eventually, his parents had agreed to find their own home, and they did, which made raising the girls a little easier without parenting input from Grandma and

Grandpa. Still, it was nice when his parents had suggested that they move back in with him after Marie had died.

The room fell into silence again. Frankie considered turning out the light after a few minutes, but Levi asked another question.

"How are we going to find Evelyn?"

Frankie took a deep breath and felt his body relax into the pillows. "I don't know. Hecate is the only one who knows where she is and if we take away her powers, we might never be able to find her."

Levi turned in his bed to face Frankie's. "So maybe you can cast a spell or something. Maybe you can even ask Anna and William to help boost it."

"A spell to do what?"

"To find Evelyn."

"No. I don't think it would work. Besides, Anna is pregnant with my father. If anything happens to her, we'd be pulled into a time paradox, where I've never been born, but she wouldn't have gotten hurt if she hadn't met me. It'd be an impossible loop."

"Then maybe William can help."

"He doesn't know who I am. And I don't think he'd even be willing to help us."

"Then tell him who you are."

"I can't."

"Why not?" There was an edge to Levi's voice.

"Because he was a big part of my life growing up," Frankie said. "And if I'm ever going to get back to my time, then I need to preserve as much of my history as possible."

"Then why can't you cast a spell on your own? You know Evelyn. You're friends with her. The call would be strong enough, wouldn't it?"

"Sure it would. Except for one problem."

"What's that?"

Frankie nodded to the corner. "My wife is standing over there looking at me."

Levi followed Frankie's gaze and saw nothing.

"I'm trying to ignore her," Frankie went on, "but she's *right there*. Tempting me. I can't shake her from my mind."

"It's just a phantom. It's not really her."

"I know that. But she looks so real. I can't get her out of my mind. Obviously, Hecate's magic is still affecting me."

Levi flopped onto his back and stared at the ceiling. He let out a long, exasperated sigh.

In the hall, they heard the creak of the floorboards as Anna or William shuffled across toward the bathroom. The sound of the door closing confirmed the activity.

"I want to thank you," Frankie said quietly.

LURED BY MAGIC

"For what?"

"For watching out for me. Guiding me through the phantom's manipulation. I definitely would've traded my soul by now if it wasn't for you."

Levi smiled. "You're welcome. But we're not out of the woods yet."

"Not by a long shot."

"If anything, our problems are worse than before."

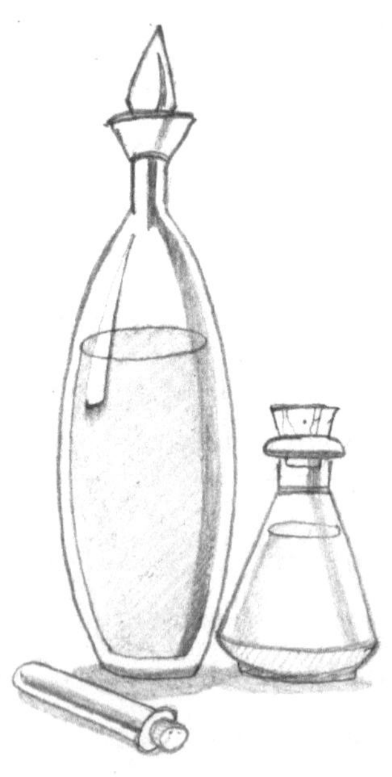

CHAPTER 32

The day had come. The date indicated in the mysterious letter left under Eddie's porch. He paced the floor in his kitchen, contemplating. He had been thinking hard about what to do over the last couple of days—going back and forth on whether or not to cast the spell.

He wasn't an overtly religious man, but some lingering guilt made him question casting an unknown ritual left under his porch by his former realtor. That was, if it truly was Frankie who had left the note in the first place.

Eddie wanted to believe that it was Frankie, but why would he choose a former client to leave the message?

Sure, they had been friendly, but they hadn't been *friends*. And to reveal such a secretive part of his life?

Again, how could Eddie know that it was the truth? Maybe it was a joke. Maybe there were people outside his window right now watching him.

He stepped to the windows and peered around the curtains, but didn't see anyone. A lone car stopped at the stop sign at the corner, then proceeded on. Otherwise, there was no activity outside.

Eddie looked down at the spell ingredients laid out on the kitchen table. He had read through the instructions a thousand times, so he knew just what to do, but was he really capable of doing this? Witchcraft?

The words of Father Thompson scared him. Witchcraft was only okay in the fictional sense. And maybe that's what this was. Then again, maybe it wasn't. He worried that he would mistakenly cross a moral line that he couldn't return from. After his conversation with Father Thompson, he had read and reread the letter and couldn't see any mention of worshipping any other deities other than God, but if the power in the spell didn't come from a deity, then where did it come from?

Eddie cracked his knuckles as he paced the room. He wished there was someone else he could talk to about this. Someone who wouldn't think he was crazy. For a brief moment, he debated whether he could go to

Frankie's house—maybe see if Frankie was there himself. That would resolve all of this.

But he'd tried that before. Instead, Frankie's daughter had deflected any questions. He remembered the look on Samantha's face. Worry. Fear. But also determination. She had put up a wall and was not about to let anyone pass through her barrier. All in the name of concern for her father.

Eddie plopped down in a chair at the end of the table and leaned back. He studied the items again. He wanted to help Frankie. He wanted to help Frankie's daughters. Reunite a family, even if he never saw their reunion for himself. Eddie knew all too well what it was like to tear apart a family after his own divorce.

What was the worst that would happen if he cast the spell? If he suffered eternal damnation for reuniting a family, then so be it. If it was a joke, then the only person who would see it was himself.

Eddie sucked in a shuddering breath. He had made his decision.

CHAPTER 33

Frankie lay awake and watched the shadows of the trees on the ceiling flicker in the gentle breeze outside. He fought the urge to drift off to sleep, which wasn't as difficult as he thought it'd be. His mind was swirling with worries and debates and schemes.

There were so many people in 1924 who were risking their lives to save his. To help him return to his family. People who didn't owe him anything. Not according to him, anyway. Even the ones who were a part of his family didn't have any responsibility to put his life over their own.

And yet they were.

If he allowed them to do that, then what did that say

about him? And what would that mean for his future?

Frankie waited until he heard Levi's deep breathing and knew that his friend was asleep. Then he slipped out of bed and carefully stepped across the wood floors.

The bright side about being the 20s was that the house didn't creak nearly as much as it did in the 80s. He didn't have to worry about alerting Levi to his departure as he snuck out of the room.

Downstairs, he pulled on one of William's jackets and stepped into the chilly air. There was something about having his grandfather's coat around him that made him feel safer, even though he was traveling in the dark alone and directly toward the very hands that he and Levi came to William and Anna's to avoid.

Frankie managed to take the last trolley ride back into town and back toward the intersection of W 27th and Raspberry streets. Back to where they had first encountered Hecate.

On the edge of town, the dark was nearly absolute. Just as it had been outside of William and Anna's house. But after venturing back into the heart of the city and then back out again, the starkness of the evening was blinding to Frankie.

He stood in the center of the intersection, hoping that Hecate would appear. He needed to make the deal before anyone could talk him out of it. Before anyone could

Frankie squinted his eyes and studied Tommy's reactions. The terror. The haggard look on his face. Seeing things that weren't there.

Tommy was being targeted by his own phantom.

Frankie broke out into a run and quickly closed the distance between them.

"Hey." Frankie's parental instincts kicked in. He dropped to his knees and wrapped Tommy in a hug from behind. The close contact—the physical touch—would hopefully help to break Tommy out of whatever mental torment he was going through. "It's okay. Whatever you're seeing, it's not real. It's meant to make you go crazy. Tommy—wake up from this daydream. It's me. It's Frankie, from the restaurant."

Despite Frankie's best efforts, Tommy continued to shake. Even as Frankie shushed him.

"Shh. Hey, look at me." He held Tommy's chin and forced the younger man to look in his direction. Even when he did, his eyes were glassy, unfocused. "Tommy, it's not real. Whatever you're seeing, it's not really there."

"You're wasting your time."

Frankie looked up to the center of the crossroads where a shadow now stood. Even without seeing her, Frankie knew who it was.

Hecate.

CHAPTER 34

As Evelyn followed Tommy up Raspberry Street, she saw the shadow in the crossroads long before she noticed Tommy's phantom. Somehow, she knew that it was Frankie even before he showed himself to Tommy.

"Frankie," she said with the hint of a smile on her face. It was the most enthusiasm that she could muster. All hope in her had vanished. Her will to live was fading, as much as it was in her host.

Before Tommy noticed Frankie, the phantom appeared. Once again in the form of his father, who continued to belittle Tommy.

"Look at you, walking home in the middle of the

night to an empty house because nobody likes you enough to stick around," his father spat. "You were supposed to do better. You were supposed to be the future. And now? Look at you. You're pathetic. A disgrace."

Evelyn wished she could plug her ears and not listen to any of it, but she couldn't. As much as Tommy was hearing it, so was she.

The only difference was, it didn't have quite the same impact on her as it did Tommy simply because she didn't have the personal connection to Tommy's father. But still, it hurt to hear it.

Even as Frankie rushed over to Tommy and tried to stir him from the terror, Tommy's phantom father continued to drawl on.

"You work a deadbeat job because you have no skills and nobody has any faith in you to train you. You're stupid. You're useless. You're serving no one with your life. What are you really contributing to the world? You wash dishes and serve tables for a living. Can't even make an honest wage. Can't even find a woman to carry on our name. Not that it would matter. If you ever became a father, your kid would be a disappointment just like you are."

Evelyn thought her head was going to explode. The world around her seemed to fade away as she sunk lower into her depression, which was feeding off of Tommy's own depression. He was nearly completely gone. Almost too far to return to any sense of normalcy, even if they could fix any of the impacts effecting him.

In the chaos, Evelyn noticed another figure in the crossroads. A shadow at first, but as she grew closer, she saw that it was Hecate. And she was talking to Frankie.

There was no hope left in Evelyn's soul, but she did believe that Frankie was the key to saving them. To freeing them. And it needed to end where it had started: with Hecate.

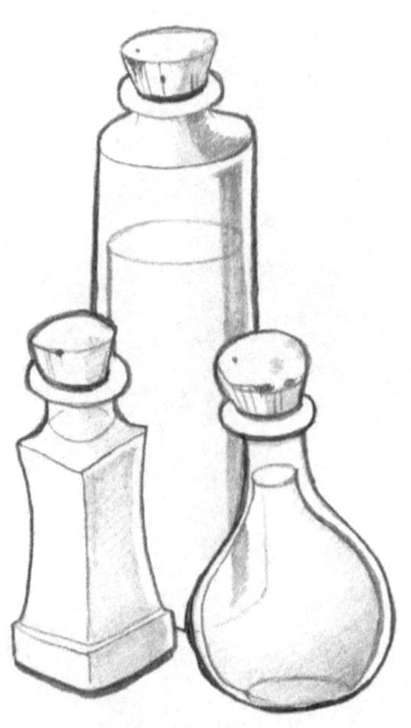

CHAPTER 35

Hecate stood, in all of her intimidating glory, in the shadows of the evening. "That poor fool is too far gone."

"He's not a fool." Frankie slowly released Tommy and rose to his feet. "You've been tormenting him. Torturing him. Just like you've been trying to do to me."

She laughed. "Please. Don't try to act tough. I know that my phantom has been working her way into your mind. If it wasn't for your silly mortal friend, then I would've had your soul by now."

The witch opened his mouth to reply, but the sight of Tommy rising to his feet and running toward his house distracted him.

Lured by Magic

"Enough of that," Hecate said. "That's not why I'm here. I wanted to let you know that my proposal is still on the table. Your soul for the chance to go back to your time. Now that it's just the two of us, we can finally come to an agreement."

"I need an assurance that Zanabar will actually take me back to 1984. To the one that I remember leaving, not an alternate one. Otherwise, there is no deal."

Hecate shrugged. "The only thing I'm able to do is to bring back Zanabar to this time. Which I've done. After that, it's up to the two of you to hash out the details."

Frankie was shaking his head before she even finished. "No. I need a guarantee."

"Would you like me to summon Zanabar here to talk to you?"

Frankie turned toward the direction Tommy had run off to. He didn't like it that he was alone in the middle of the night. Not in the state that he was in.

Tommy had been the perfect distraction. Up until Frankie had seen him, Frankie had every intention of coming to the crossroads to trade in his soul for a trip back to 1984. Thankfully, he had changed his mind. "You do what you want," Frankie told Hecate. "I have other things I need to deal with."

"Wait!" Hecate groaned. "I can work something out with Zanabar. I have a few souls that I've collected through the years that might be of interest to him. Or rather, their powers would be. Former witches, you know?"

"I need a guarantee," Frankie demanded.

"All right! All right!" she droned. "I'll make sure Zanabar agrees to take you back to 1984. The one that you remember."

Frankie nodded, contemplating the consequences of his decision. But he knew it was the right choice. His soul in exchange for putting an end to this was a trade he was willing to make.

"So do we have a deal?" Hecate asked. "I need an official confirmation."

The witch studied her for a moment, then closed the distance between them in two steps and reached for her free hand. "Deal."

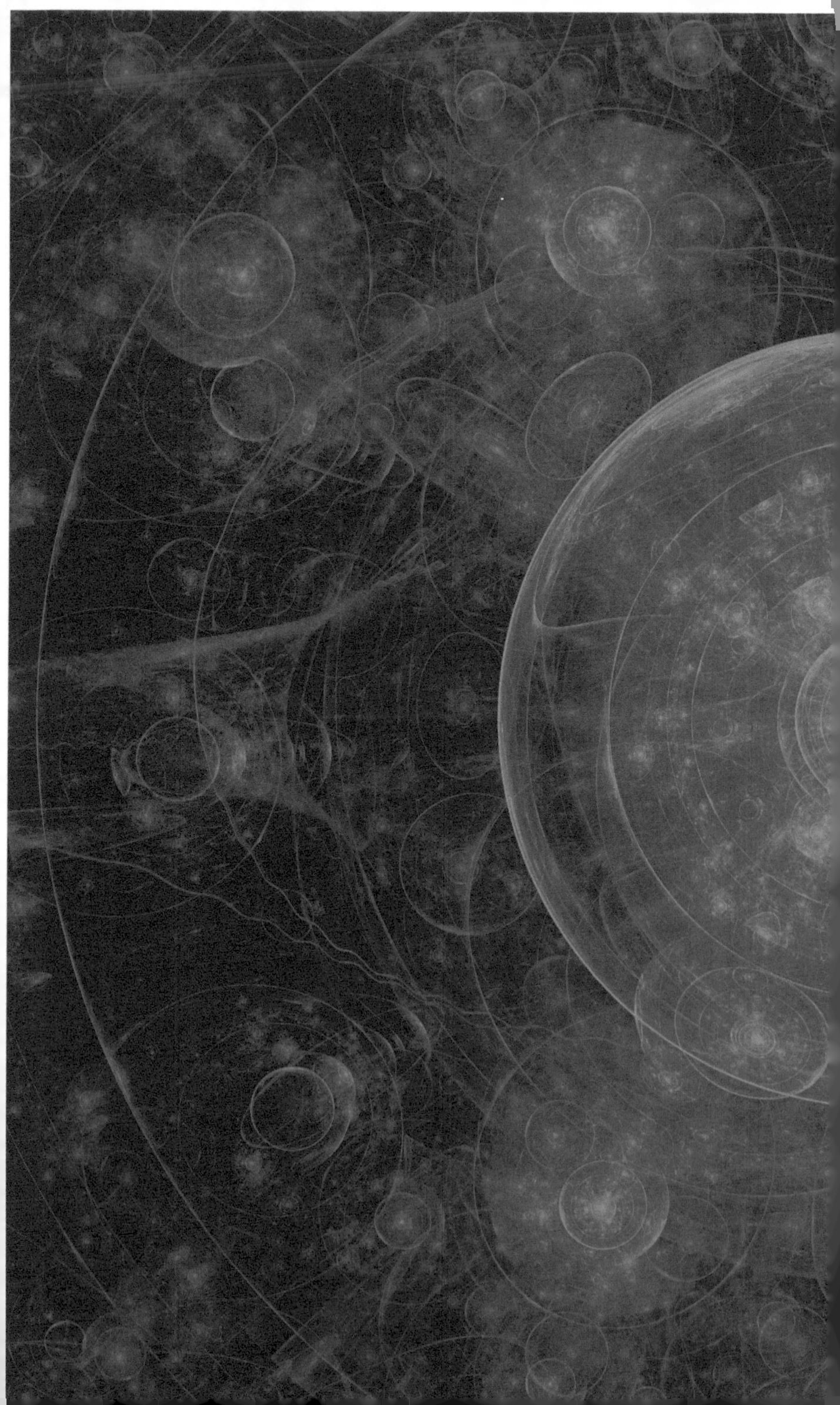

CHAPTER 36

The restfulness of the twin bed in Anna's guest bedroom had run its course. Levi found himself tossing and turning shortly after he fell asleep, unable to get comfortable.

As he rolled over once again, he cracked his eyes open to see if Frankie was having as difficult a time sleeping as he was. Across the room, the second bed lay empty.

"Frankie?" Levi sat up to get a better look. He waited for half a beat, trying to listen for any sign that his friend had simply run to the bathroom. But the bedroom door was closed and the house was silent.

Letting out a heavy sigh, Levi got to his feet. There

was only one place Frankie could've gone and it wasn't good.

He rushed to pull on his shoes and a heavier coat, then hurried down the stairs and out into the chilly night air.

"Can't leave well enough alone," he muttered to himself as he marched down the darkened dirt road. "Has to always go and play the hero."

He had forgotten to check the time on his way out of the house, but Levi was hoping that if he made it to Cherry Street that he could catch a trolley back into town. It was a stretch, but otherwise it meant walking all the way to the crossroads where they had first encountered Hecate, which would take him the better part of the night. And there wasn't a doubt in Levi's mind that that's where his friend had gone.

As he crossed one of the streets that intersected Arlington, a shadow appeared suddenly in the middle of the intersection.

Levi's heart nearly skipped a beat and he froze in place. "Hecate?"

"Yes, it's me," she said. "Consider this a courtesy call on behalf of your witch friend."

"What are you talking about?"

"You're too late," she said. "Frankie Walker has already agreed to trade in his soul."

Levi felt a sinking feeling in the pit of his stomach. "He did?"

Even in the darkness, Hecate's smirk was visible. "Yes."

"I don't believe you." Truth be told he didn't *want* to believe her. But then, Frankie had mentioned it before, and if it wasn't for Levi talking him off the ledge, he would've already gone through with it before now. Maybe that was why he had snuck out. So that Levi couldn't stop him this time. Maybe his wife's phantom had led him straight toward Hecate. "Where is he?" Levi demanded, suddenly angry. At Hecate; at Frankie—he wasn't sure.

"Oh, I don't know," she said. "I would assume he's on his way back to your hideout here. Which, by the way, wasn't hard to find. Bloodlines and all. Anyway, I can travel via crossroads. Your friend cannot. It takes him longer."

Levi didn't have time to wait for Frankie to get back. They needed to cancel the deal before Hecate could make good on her end of the bargain.

"I want to propose a counter-deal," he blurted.

She laughed. "Well, that's a first. I've never had a mortal offer their own deal for me. Usually I choose my victims myself and negotiate my own terms. But I'm in a good mood. I'll entertain your idea. What is it you would like to offer?"

"I trade in my soul in exchange for Frankie's. He keeps his soul—and his deal with Zanabar to return to 1984—and you take my soul instead."

"And why would I agree to that? A witch's soul is more valuable than a lousy mortal's."

"But without Frankie, I have no way of finding Evelyn," Levi said. "I know you had something to do with her disappearance. It's somehow connected to Tommy too, who you're also hoping will trade in his soul. By swapping my soul for Frankie's, you may be losing a witch, but you're gaining two mortals and an oracle. There's no way I'd be able to save Evelyn before Tommy succumbs to his demons."

"Phantoms," Hecate corrected. She tapped her chin as she considered. "Hmm. You raise an interesting point. Color me intrigued."

"So?" Levi asked. "Is it a deal?"

Hecate studied him a moment longer. Then, with a shrug, she said, "What the hell? I suppose you have a deal."

CHAPTER 37

- FRIDAY, OCTOBER 17, 1924 -

Moments after Hecate had disappeared in the center of the crossroads at 27th and Raspberry, Frankie stood alone in the darkness and wondered if he had made the right decision. He wished that he could return to his time with his soul intact, but he also wished that he could bring Levi and Evelyn with him, which still wouldn't fit because they'd be displaced from their own time. There was no perfect solution.

It was as if Frankie didn't fit anywhere in the timeline anymore. If he was back in 1984, he'd be missing his friends from 1924, and if he stayed in 1924, he'd be missing out on his daughters' lives. But maybe it was for the best that he disappear soulless. At least that way he wouldn't live with regrets.

He sighed and turned in the direction of Tommy's house. If nothing else, while he still had a soul, he needed to check in on him. Make sure that Hecate didn't take his soul before she was able to take Frankie's. He wouldn't put it past the old hag to take both of theirs and go back on the deal. After all, once his soul was gone, who was going to stop her from doing what she wanted?

As he turned, though, a particular house on the corner caught his eye. He had noticed it the last couple times that he had been to this intersection, but it wasn't until now that it's possibilities finally clicked with him.

He had sold it to someone in 1984. Or—*will* sell it to someone. The tenses confused him still, but either way, he had a personal connection to the house—and its future occupant.

Frankie darted down the street toward Tommy's house. He burst through the door, which was left ajar.

"Tommy?" Frankie called out, but heard no answer.

His eyes scanned the room and he saw Tommy curled up in the corner of the living room with his knees tucked against his chest. He quietly whimpered.

"Phantom," Frankie murmured to himself. But he had no time to comfort Tommy just yet. He needed to get a piece of paper and a pen.

Darting to the kitchen, Frankie searched through

cupboards and drawers until he found an old blank shopping list stationary and something to write with. There were two spells he needed to come up with on the spot. Both had been ruminating in his mind for some time. He only hoped that they would be as effective as he needed them to be.

He bent over onto the kitchen counter and scrawled out a letter to Eddie McDonald, his former client. He started with the note first, trying to convey the urgency and the accuracy without giving too much information away. Then he started listing the instructions and the ingredients needed to perform the ritual. Frankie wasn't sure if he'd be able to get everything together himself, but if he had someone else casting the spell—even someone mortal—then maybe the energies would align and allow for the magic to progress the way that he intended.

When he was finished writing, he reread the note and then folded it once. It was a long shot—a *very* long shot— but it was one he had to take. If it didn't work, his soul would burn in hell for eternity.

Exiting the kitchen, he paused to look at Tommy, who had slipped to the floor and now slept restlessly on the hardwood. But at least he was alive and safe. For now.

Darting back out into the cold, Frankie returned to

the house on the corner and debated his options for where to place the note. It would need to be somewhere secure for sixty years. Somewhere that Tommy would look, but no one else would. And it would need to be outside. There was no way Frankie was going to get arrested for breaking into someone's house in the middle of the night.

There was a small gap beneath the riser board on the bottom porch step. Frankie dropped to his knees and folded the note again, then slipped it in the small space between the wooden step and the ground.

Hopefully this makes it sixty years, he thought to himself.

With one last glimpse at the house, he turned and left, ready for the long walk back to Anna's.

CHAPTER 38

- FRIDAY, OCTOBER 17, 1924 -

Evelyn barely even noticed when Frankie walked into Tommy's house. Her spirit had been so badly degraded. Rather, *Tommy's* spirit had been so badly degraded, and since they had a psychic connection, her's was effected too.

She knew all of this, and yet she couldn't shake the overwhelming sense of despair. Of hopelessness. The complete withdrawal of a will to live.

So when Frankie stepped into Tommy's house and glanced in his direction, Evelyn wasn't happy. She wasn't excited. She wasn't hopeful. She was indifferent. Because what difference could his presence make if he couldn't see her, hear her, or even sense her in any way?

And the longer she spent tied to Tommy's psyche, the weaker she became. Soon, she would be completely swallowed up in his emptiness. Lost in the ether, and never thought about again.

Frankie disappeared into the kitchen. Evelyn didn't even try to follow him to figure out what he was doing. Not only because of her lack of energy, but also because Tommy's phantom—Tommy's father—loomed over him, sneering and throwing insults at Tommy.

"You're pathetic."

"You have brought shame to our family name."

"There's no point in you wasting anyone else's time anymore."

"You'd be better off dead."

Each statement struck Tommy and, in turn, Evelyn as well. They were like physical lashings, each blow more devastating than the last.

And even though the words weren't directed at Evelyn herself, she still felt them. Still felt a moral obligation to protect Tommy as best as she could. Be the presence that would stand by him until the end. Unlike everyone else who had left him in his life.

So she laid next to Tommy and held him as the phantom continued to berate him. It was all she could do.

Eventually, Frankie exited the kitchen and paused as he took in Tommy's curled up form on the floor. He was within arm's reach of Evelyn. It was quiet, except for the phantom. If there was ever a time to try to reach out to Frankie, now was the time.

"Frankie," Evelyn croaked. But there was no power to her voice whatsoever. It was like trying to shout in a dream. Stifled. Weak.

Her friend didn't even flinch at all at the sound of her voice. She cleared her throat and prepared to try again, but a second phantom made her shrink back toward Tommy.

Frankie's phantom. And she was beautiful. Just like the woman Frankie had described in one of the rare moments that he had talked about his wife before all of this mess started.

Maybe Frankie would be joining Evelyn soon. Maybe she wouldn't be alone.

That hope was quickly squashed. If Frankie was being haunted by a phantom, that could only end in his eternal damnation.

And there was nothing she could do to stop it from happening.

Chapter 39

Hecate snapped her fingers. Suddenly, she and Levi were in the company of Frankie, Tommy, and Zanabar, who all stood in the center of the crossroads with her.

All three of the newcomers looked startled, but Frankie quickly stepped away from Hecate and Zanabar, pulling Tommy with him.

"What's going on?" Zanabar asked.

"It's dark. It's late. I thought this would be the perfect meeting place." Hecate turned to face Frankie. "So! Change of plans. Your friend, here, has agreed to trade *his* soul in exchange for yours."

Frankie whirled around on Levi. "You didn't!"

Lured by Magic

Levi wouldn't meet his eyes. The somber silence was interrupted after a moment with Tommy's wails at the sight of his phantom.

Hecate rolled her eyes. "Oh, would you *shut up*!" She waved a hand in front of him and a few seconds later he stopped.

Frankie turned back to the former god. "What did you do to him?"

"Don't worry. I sent his phantom away. If anything, I'm helping him."

The witch looked over and studied Tommy. His eyes seemed wide and he looked around before settling back into himself and burying his head in his hands. There was nothing they could do for him at the moment, and if his phantom was gone, at least he wasn't in anymore pain.

Facing Hecate again, Frankie said, "You can't accept Levi's offer."

"I already did."

"He doesn't know what it means!"

"Of course I do," Levi chimed in.

Frankie ignored him and kept his eyes on the former goddess. "Reverse it."

Hecate was growing angry. "No. And actually, this works in your favor. You get to keep your deal with Zanabar to return to your time *and* you get to keep your soul as well. I don't understand why you're fighting this."

Frankie turned to Levi. "Why would you do this?"

"You're my best friend." Levi's voice broke and he had tears in his eyes. "You've changed my life. Helped me out numerous times when you didn't have to. Saved my life over and over again. I'd do anything for you."

Frankie held his friend's stare. He was at a complete loss for words. A part of him wanted to accept it all and just return to his time—and return to his daughters—and forget everything that had happened during his stint in the 20s.

But another part—a larger part—knew that that wasn't right. He couldn't let someone else trade their life so that he could have one. Levi truly didn't owe him anything.

"All right, that's enough," Hecate cut in. "You two are worse than some of the married couples I have to separate. Sheesh." She turned to Zanabar and gestured at Frankie. "Well? Go on. Get started."

Frankie's eyes flickered between the two of them. In a moment of panic, he reached for a copy of one of the spells that he had written back at Tommy's house and began reciting.

LURED BY MAGIC

In the late-night darkness, a blinding light shone from Frankie, radiating out from where he stood in the crossroads. Everyone turned away from the light—even Tommy—and used their hands to shield their eyes from the brightness.

Just as quickly as it had come, the light vanished, and the after effects left everyone seeing stars.

As everyone blinked to clear their vision, the first thing they each noticed was that Frankie had disappeared.

CHAPTER 40

Immediately after having cast the spell, Frankie wasn't sure that it had even worked. He watched as everyone in the crossroads shielded their eyes, then looked to the spot where he stood.

He raised his hands, ready to use his power, but stopped when he heard Zanabar say, "Where did he go?"

Frankie patted chest and looked down at himself. He hadn't gone invisible; hadn't become transparent. He could still see and feel feel his body. And yet, none of the rest of them could see him. That must've meant that his spell had worked.

Looking around, he took a quick inventory of everyone. There was Hecate, Zanabar, Levi, Tommy, and…an older man who looked angry. Mean, almost. He had a shadowy aura to him that he'd seen whenever Marie showed up, which told Frankie that he was a phantom. The way he loomed over Tommy confirmed that.

Beside Tommy, Evelyn lay—nearly unrecognizable—in the dirt road.

"Evelyn," Frankie said under his breath. He took a step toward her, but stopped when the sight of his own phantom blocked his path.

Marie.

"Frankie," she said. "Come home with me. Let's be together again. Only you can make it so."

Even with the shadowy aura radiating from her and the knowledge that she wasn't real, Frankie still couldn't quite reconcile those facts with his mind. He was tempted to grab her, hold her, break down and sob at the sight of her out of loneliness.

But he kept his resolve. The phantom wasn't real. He needed to remember that.

"Don't you love me?" Marie pleaded. "Why don't you want to be with me?"

Frankie stepped around Marie, fighting every urge to wrap her in his arms. He rushed to the oracle on the ground, this time calling out to her again. "Evelyn! I'm here to help!"

Her head picked up in surprise and she looked at him.

Once again, though, he stopped before he could reach her.

"Before your friend has a chance to interfere, I think it's time I cashed in on that deal we made," Hecate said to Levi. She held up the lantern in her hand to Levi.

"No!" Frankie waved his hand at the lantern, sending it crashing to the ground and cracking. "Levi, run!"

He wasn't convinced that his friend had heard him, but after another second—and a threatening look from Zanabar—Levi spun and raced in the opposite direction.

On his way, Levi reached for Tommy and pulled him to his feet. Hooking his arm around his shoulder, he nearly dragged him down one of the darkened streets with houses that were still being constructed.

Frankie spun around as they left, noticing that not only was Tommy's phantom following them, but so was Evelyn. It was as if she were being dragged against her will as Tommy moved.

Zanabar turned to Hecate. "First, you make deals that involve me without consulting me, and *now* the collateral you've offered up to me is gone. Find him or I'll take you instead!"

Hecate raised her hand above her shattered lantern

and called it back into her grasp. As it rose from the ground, the broken pieces of glass reassembled and the flame relit, as if it hadn't ever been broken.

Walking casually, she stepped in the direction Levi and Tommy had gone, then waved her hand back in Zanabar's direction. A perimeter of light rose up momentarily around the crossroads, then dissipated.

"Nobody gives me an ultimatum, honey," Hecate said to the sorcerer as she walked on down the street.

"What have you done?" Zanabar called after her.

"You're trapped," she said. "For now. Just until I need you again."

Zanabar's hands came out from under his cloak. With a flick of his wrists and a twirl of his fingers, he conjured a ball of zapping electricity and sent it hurtling in Hecate's direction. The electric ball soared through the air until it reached the edge of the crossroads, where it hit an invisible force field and ricocheted back toward Zanabar. He dodged it, just barely, and the attack hit the force field on the other side, where it faded and dissipated, leaving smoke lingering in the air.

"Don't hurt yourself." Hecate sneered. "See you in a bit, dear." Ignoring Zanabar's threats, and shouts for her to come back, Hecate started down the darkened dirt road.

Frankie broke out into a run and chased his friends

down. Levi was struggling to pull Tommy along with any sense of speed. Finally, he gave up and decided to hide instead. Levi climbed a small embankment and backed into the branches of a pine tree, pulling Tommy along with him.

Frankie ran to meet up with them, but felt his energy depleting.

As Hecate drew nearer, Frankie used his magic to make a tree branch fall across the street. She nearly stepped over it. He moved a rock in front of her, but she stepped around it. Unfazed by it all.

The more he exerted himself, the more he felt tired. Exhausted.

Worse, the more effort he put out, the less he cared about helping Levi. About reversing his spell and escaping the alternate plane he was in.

It was as if this second dimension were killing his soul.

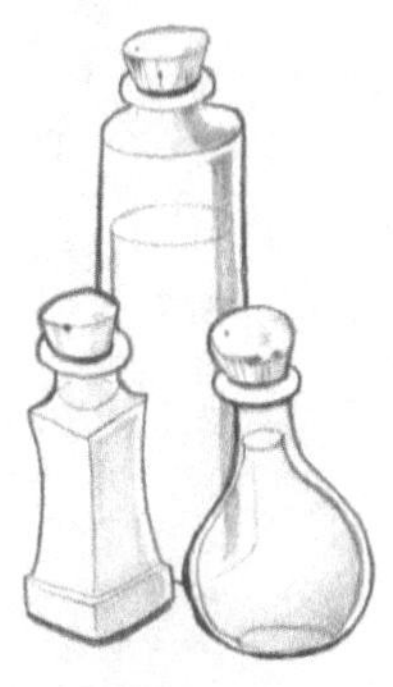

CHAPTER 41

Evelyn watched from her hiding place with Tommy and Levi as Frankie weakened with the exertion of his powers—and his body. He stood in the center of the street as Hecate loomed closer. In the shadows, their proximity had not been realized to each other yet. There was still time for Frankie to escape.

"Frankie!" Evelyn called out.

His head swiveled toward the sound of her voice.

For the first time in a long time, Evelyn felt hope.

"Evelyn? Where are you?"

"Right here! I'm stuck—trapped in a psychological connection with Tommy. It's been a couple days."

Frankie still couldn't place where her voice was

coming from, but he followed the sound of it. "Hang on. I'm coming to help."

"I have to stay near Tommy," she explained. "I can't control anything within the real world. It's like I'm on an alternate plane or something."

"That's exactly where we are. I cast a spell so that I could be on the same plane as my phantom." Frankie climbed up a small embankment and into some overgrowth. "I thought I could stop Hecate by stopping my phantom. Levi traded in his soul to save mine. If I can stop Hecate, then I can save Levi's soul."

"He traded in his soul?"

"Not yet. I don't think she got to him. But the deal's been made." Frankie huffed. "I can't…it's hard…to breathe."

"It's this plane," Evelyn said from nearby. "I've been growing weaker the longer I've been here. It's like this alternate world is draining my will to live. That's probably how Hecate gets her victims to agree to trade in their souls. She tortures them."

Frankie was quiet at first, although the rustling of the weeds around them signaled his movement. "We're going to get out of here. We just need to save Levi first."

"Too bad he can't hear your master plan," Evelyn said. "If he could hear us, we could work together to figure out a way out of here."

Frankie stepped into Evelyn's view and she reached out and touched his shoulder so they knew where the other was in the darkness. Just the sense of touching someone who knew that she was there gave her more hope than she'd had since she cast the spell to connect to Tommy.

Frankie pulled Evelyn into a hug. "It's so good to see you!"

His arms wrapped around her warmed her spirit. Suddenly, she felt more alive—and had more energy—than she'd had in a couple days.

"It's good to be seen." She pulled him tighter to her.

The witch pulled away. "We don't have a lot of time."

Evelyn nodded to Frankie's left.

Levi was on the move. Slowly, quietly, at first. But then Tommy groaned.

"You won't be able to hide forever," Hecate called to them from the street.

Her words made Levi move faster, pulling Tommy along with him and throwing all possibility of stealth out the window.

Evelyn was dragged along with them and Frankie hurried to keep up.

"Don't use your power," she warned. "It'll only weaken you. Wait until we're closer. When we'll really need it."

"Okay." Frankie struggled to keep up with the group's pace. He couldn't imagine using his power on top of it.

Eventually, Levi made it to the next street that ran parallel to Arlington. He hesitated, eyeing the crossroads, then cut through the yard of the recently-constructed house. Unlike many of the other houses in the area, this one had landscaping and a white picket fence outlining the perimeter of the property.

"Come on, Tommy," Levi encouraged. "We can do this. Up and over the fence." He heaved, but Tommy was nothing but dead weight and collapsed against the fence.

"She's gaining on us." Worry crept into Frankie's voice.

"Gate," Evelyn muttered.

Confused, Frankie looked around until his eyes landed on the opening through the fence down a few feet. It was hard to see in the darkness.

"Gate!" Frankie echoed. "Gate!"

But Levi couldn't hear him and continued to struggle to get Tommy to climb over the fence.

Frankie flicked his fingers and the gate softly moved. It was barely a blip, but it made enough noise that it caught Levi's attention.

"Better idea, Tommy." Levi hauled him down to the

gate, but when he swung it open Hecate suddenly appeared.

She sneered down at them. "Doorways are my mode of transportation, dear."

"Damn," Frankie swore to himself. He should've seen that coming, but he wasn't thinking straight. Not with how tired he was.

"Frankie, we have to do something!" Evelyn cried out.

"There's nothing you can do!" Hecate said to her, then turned back on Levi. "It's time to pay the piper!" She loomed over him and held up her lantern. Levi froze where he was as his soul slowly began to exit his body.

"Levi!" Frankie yelled, but it was no use. All he could do was watch as his friend's soul was ripped from his body. And all for Frankie. Levi was nonmagical. He was happy. There was no reason for him to be trading his soul in at all.

"That is the last time that you contain me!" Zanabar suddenly roared from beside Hecate.

The sudden appearance of the sorcerer broke her concentration and Levi's soul—which was halfway between his body and her lantern—returned back to Levi and he slumped to the ground.

Frankie ran to his friend and tried to reach out to him, but his hand simply passed right through him.

Lured by Magic

"Levi! Get up! Come on! You have to run or she'll—"

Instinctively, Frankie ducked out of the way as a lightning bolt soared over his head as Zanabar attacked Hecate.

In return, she summoned an army of phantoms—including both Frankie's and Tommy's—to attack Zanabar. He, of course, couldn't see any of it, but Frankie did.

"Levi," Frankie tried again as his friend started to rouse. "Do you have the potion? Is it in your pocket?"

"Frankie, he can't hear you," Evelyn said from Tommy's side.

"I have to try!" He turned back to Levi. "Remember, we made it with Anna back at the house? Right after she said we could spend the night."

That was the one saving grace from all of this. This whole ordeal could've been happening in Anna's house where she would've been vulnerable and William would've been clueless and unprepared for an attack. At least Frankie's grandparents—and his unborn father— were safe.

"Levi, you have to listen to me!" Frankie called out. "Use the potion!" His voice strained as he shouted.

Meanwhile, the fight between Hecate and Zanabar grew deadlier as they each hurled attacks at one another, coming closer and closer to Levi and Tommy. For the moment, however, the phantoms seemed focused on Zanabar and not on Frankie or Tommy, and already Frankie felt more energetic than he had before.

"Get up!" Again, Frankie reached for his friend. This time, his hand landed on Levi's shoulder. The connection astounded Frankie for a second, but then he took advantage of the moment. "Use the potion!"

Levi sat up, apparently hearing Frankie's call. He looked around, confused, but Frankie called out again.

"Just throw it!"

Fishing in his pocket, Levi raised the vial and waited until Hecate drew nearer, distracted. Then, when she was close enough, he hurled the potion at her. It crashed open on impact and the contents drained onto her clothing, seeping in and reaching her skin.

She continued to move about, controlling her phantoms, until a light swirled around her before quickly vanishing. A moment later, Hecate's movements resulted in nothing. No control over phantoms. No deflecting of Zanabar's attacks. No magic.

The disgraced goddess stopped and studied her hands, then looked to Zanabar.

"What did you do?"

The sorcerer turned to Levi, then his eyes traveled to Frankie.

"He can see us?" Frankie asked Evelyn.

"*I* can see you too," Levi said.

Frankie smiled at his oracle friend. "We're back?"

"We're back!" she returned the smile, although she was weak.

"Let's get the hell out of here!" Levi said.

Frankie pulled Levi to his feet and rushed over to Evelyn and Tommy.

"Maybe the power-stripping potion removed her hold on us too?" Evelyn considered.

"Or maybe it's because once her power was gone, then the phantoms were completely ripped from existence as well," Frankie offered. "And if there were no phantoms, there was nothing tying you to the alternate plane, and I was only there to follow you. It was a chain reaction."

"Who cares?" Levi said. "We're about to die!"

Evelyn tried to get to her feet, but fell back to the ground. "I can't get up. I'm too weak. I spent too long on that other plane."

Levi looked over his shoulder, then back to his friends. "We have to go *now*."

Frankie hooked Evelyn's arm around his neck and propped up her body with one of his arms. "Levi, you grab Tommy."

"I'm on it." Levi was already helping his friend off the ground.

"Stop them!" Hecate demanded of Zanabar.

The sorcerer looked to the group, then back to Hecate and stood by.

Frankie fished in his pocket for another spell. "Evelyn, it's you and me."

"I don't think I can do it," Evelyn said. "My magic—"

"Is enough," he cut in. "We have to at least try."

She clamped her mouth shut and nodded.

Together, the two of them recited:

> *Demon of the gate, guardian of hell,*
> *We banish you to hell with this spell.*

Hecate froze, her eyes frantically flashing between Frankie and Evelyn, and Zanabar. Then a portal opened beneath her feet and she fell into it, sending a scream echoing up from inside. The next second, the portal closed up, leaving an eerie quiet in its wake.

"Is it over?" Levi asked.

Zanabar stepped toward them and raised his hands from beneath his cloak. "No, it is not."

CHAPTER 42

Levi's heart pounded in his chest as Zanabar loomed over them. "Okay, what are we going to do?"

Frankie used his free hand to try to send Zanabar flying back with his power, but he was still too weak from his short stint in the alternate plane. The only effect his power had on Zanabar was on the same level as someone giving him a firm push on the shoulder.

"We have to go," Evelyn murmured from Frankie's side. Her body still slumped beside him.

"There's nowhere you can run," Zanabar said. "You don't have anyone left to protect you. And now, you'll finally pay for your betrayal."

Lured by Magic

The spell rolled off of Frankie's tongue. Within moments, flames shot up from Zanabar's robes.

The sorcerer turned and swatted at himself to put the magical fire out, which gave the rest of them the opportunity they needed to escape.

They moved as quickly as they could, with Evelyn and Tommy slowing them down considerably. The darkness, however, was on their side and concealed them, which helped since they didn't have speed.

"Any plan for how to stop him with your powers weakened?" Levi asked after they were a good distance away.

"I have a…contingency plan…in place," Frankie muttered between ragged breaths. He was growing tired by the urgency and carrying most of Evelyn's weight.

"Great. What is it?"

"It's a long shot," Frankie admitted. "It'll also mean…that I'm…stuck in 1924." He didn't try to hide his heavy breathing anymore.

"Is it something you can do now to get him off of our tails?" Levi asked. "Tommy's not exactly light and you sound like you've run a marathon."

Frankie tried to reach for his watch, but couldn't see

the time in the darkness. "I have to wait until midnight exactly. Which means I need to get somewhere with better lighting so I can check the time."

"It's just about midnight now," Evelyn muttered.

Both Frankie and Levi looked at her with confusion.

"Watching time pass was one of Tommy's hobbies," she explained. "There's not much to do when you live alone."

"Remind me to check in more on my employees," Levi muttered. "How long do you think we have until exactly midnight?"

"I don't know," Evelyn said. "It was about twenty minutes past eleven the last time I checked at Tommy's house. And that was maybe thirty minutes ago, so we have about—"

"Ten minutes to kill," Frankie finished.

From behind them, Zanabar threw a bolt of lightning that struck the crude dirt road and momentarily blinded the group.

"I don't think we have ten minutes!" Levi panicked.

"We have to get back to Anna's," Frankie said. "She has protection charms on the house. It won't hold him off completely, but it's better than nothing and it'll buy us some time."

"What about the risk to her baby—your father?" Levi asked.

Lured by Magic

"It's a risk we're going to have to take," Frankie said. "We have to hurry."

As Zanabar launched another lightning bolt in their direction, Frankie and Levi did their best to pick up the pace.

CHAPTER 43

"We made it!" Levi said as they walked up the front sidewalk toward Anna and William's house. He gently set Tommy down on the ground.

"Huh? What's going on?" he murmured.

"Shh," Levi soothed, crouching beside his friend. "Just lay back and try not to pay attention to anything that's happening. We'll keep you safe." He stood again and stepped toward Frankie, who was making sure Evelyn was steady on her feet. "Please help me keep my promise to him."

Frankie took a deep breath. "I'm going to try to keep us all safe."

Lured by Magic

"How much time do we have?" Evelyn asked.

With the light on the front porch of the house, Frankie could see his watch. "Only a couple more minutes."

"What's the plan?" Levi asked. "Do you have a spell? What if Zanabar comes before it's time?"

Frankie looked up and saw the figure standing at the end of the sidewalk.

Time was up.

Instinctively, Frankie stretched out his hands to protect his friends and took a small step forward.

"You decided to lure me back to your home?" Zanabar asked. "Or, should I say, *former* home?"

"This place is surrounded by protection charms," Frankie warned. "You can't come any closer."

Zanabar smiled and shot a bolt of lightning in their direction. It collided with an invisible forcefield that sent shockwaves up and around the house, like a bubble.

"See?" Levi taunted. "You can't come any closer!"

Zanabar fired another lighting bolt with similar results. Then another. And another. "I broke through Hecate's barrier. I can certainly break through yours."

With each passing blow, the protection charms seemed to be weakening until one final lightning bolt broke through the protection and right toward the group. Frankie raised his hand in time to use his power to deflect the attack.

Again, the sorcerer smiled. He sauntered toward them. "Any other magic you want to try against me?"

Frankie eyed him, anticipating any move the sorcerer might make. "Levi, tell me when it's time."

"You still have another minute," he said. "Just cast the spell now!"

"Not until it's time," Frankie said.

Zanabar raised his hand and fired a lightning bolt in their direction. Again, Frankie deflected it. Then another was fired, and another. With each new attack, Frankie managed to keep it from striking anyone.

Barely.

Each use of his power became harder, more of a struggle. If he didn't reserve his power, he'd have nothing left to cast the spell.

"You can't keep this up for much longer," Zanabar sneered.

Frankie gritted his teeth. He had a point.

Sucking in a deep breath, Frankie summoned his energy and used both hands to focus his power on Zanabar. But just before he was about to release, there were suddenly three Zanabars standing in front of him. Then three more. And then more.

Soon, it was impossible to tell which was the original

and which were the illusions.

Frankie's eyes flickered as he studied them each, then finally pinpointed one and focused his power on that Zanabar.

He was wrong.

His power did nothing. Just as quickly as the duplicates had appeared, they were suddenly all gone.

"Where'd he go?" Frankie asked.

"I don't know," Levi breathed.

"Ahh!" Tommy's screams from behind them drew everyone's attention.

Zanabar stood behind Tommy with his fist driven through Tommy's back and into his chest. With a swift motion, the sorcerer ripped Tommy's heart right out of him, leaving him to crumple to the ground.

Evelyn let out a yelp and covered her mouth to stifle it.

With a blood-soaked fist, Zanabar tossed Tommy's heart aside and leaned in close to Frankie.

As the witch eyed the sorcerer, he wondered if he was about to suffer the same fate as Tommy.

CHAPTER 44

"It's time," Levi said from behind Frankie. "Cast the spell."

"You have become a bigger pain than I would've ever thought," Zanabar told Frankie, ignoring Levi. "You were supposed to be a pawn to secure additional powers for me. I had every intention of returning you to your family, as long as you didn't ask too many questions."

"You were going to kill an innocent girl," Frankie said, thinking of Ura. "Of course you needed to be stopped."

"If I hadn't tried to claim her, she would've been hunted for the rest of her eternal life," Zanabar said.

"That's exactly what her fate had been in the 1984 that I plucked you from."

"And I put a stop to that kind of life for her."

"By doing what? Locking her away for eternity? How is that any better?"

"At least she's not being used against her will," Frankie defended. "At least she has peace."

"She still lost her life. Her freedom. How does that make you any different from me?"

"Thirty seconds left." Levi's eyes darted between his watch and his friend. "Frankie, cast the spell before it's too late!"

"Don't listen to Zanabar," Evelyn said. "He's only trying to confuse you. Manipulate you."

"And *you've* somehow been a bigger pain as well." Zanabar turned his attention to the oracle, who cowered at his tone. "You were nothing but a barroom novelty before I brought the witch to this time."

"That was your own doing," Frankie said. He gestured to Tommy's body, which lay on the ground. "And now look what you've done. You need to be stopped, Zanabar!"

"And then what will you do, one I'm gone? I'm the last hope you have of seeing your family."

"Ten seconds!"

"That may be true," Frankie said, "but if I have to

give up seeing my family again to make sure your torment ends, then so be it."

He didn't need to pull out the spell. He had been memorizing it ever since he first crafted it.

Spanning the energies across all time,
I call on the power of the divine.
Rid this evil from the future and past,
Take him after this spell has been cast.

Chapter 45

- **Wednesday, October 17, 1984** -

Eddie paced around his kitchen table. All the ingredients for the spell were laid out, ready to be executed. But he was still going back and forth, debating whether he should go through with it. Not only was he afraid of looking like a fool, but he was afraid of what sort of higher power might interfere — or damn him for it later.

He thought of Father Thompson's words. He was only helping out a friend, which the church fully supported. Then again, how could he be sure that the note was really written by the Frankie Walker that he knew? It was a common enough name. It could've been anybody who wrote that note.

LURED BY MAGIC

He glanced at the time. It was two minutes until midnight. The note said to cast the spell at exactly midnight. He had to make a decision soon.

Eddie sat down at the table and blinked several times, feeling his eyes burning. His body was sore and tired from a long week at work. Not to mention the stress of mulling all of this over during the last couple days. The thought came to him that he could just go to bed and forget the whole thing.

But would that really be the end of it? Wouldn't he regret not throwing some ingredients together and saying a few words, just in case? What if he found out later that a simple rhyme, coupled with a few herbs that he had already purchased, would make the world of a difference for Frankie.

The hands on the clock ticked over to midnight. It was now or never.

Taking a deep breath, Eddie stood and began to put together the ingredients listed. There weren't too many. Three herbs—yarrow flower, thyme, and pennyroyal—and a specifically-colored candle—black—pointed to the north side of the bowl full of herbs.

He lifted the note with a shaking hand and began to recite. He started once, then stopped to clear his throat. The nerves had made his voice dry and irritated.

Clearing it, he sounded like himself as he recited the spell.

Spanning the energies across all time,
I call on the power of the divine.
Rid this evil from the future and past,
Take him after this spell has been cast.

As soon as he finished the words, he waited for something to happen. Some spark of light, or cracking of windows, or a beast to arrive to tear out his heart. Or worse, laughter and heckling.

Instead, there was nothing. No sound. No fire. No light.

Nothing.

The worry and stress Eddie had felt was immediately replaced with embarrassment. How could he be so stupid as to fall for such an obvious prank? It was a good thing he was alone. Nobody would be able to torment him for this later.

He blew out the candle and set it on the fireplace mantle in the living room, then returned to the kitchen where he promptly dumped the bowl full of herbs into the trash. He stuck the dish in the sink, tossed the note in the trash, and turned out the lights.

As Eddie lay down to bed, he stared up at the

shadows that were cast on the ceiling from the streetlight, and vowed to never mention any of this to anyone. Ever. He only hoped that the few people he had mentioned it to already would forget it just as he intended to do himself.

CHAPTER 46

There was a pause after Frankie had finished the spell, where everyone waited in anticipation.

Zanabar smiled and opened his mouth to speak, but stopped when they were suddenly bathed in light from a portal that opened right above the sorcerer's head.

"No! Your magic isn't enough to defeat me!" Zanabar cried out. "I'm too powerful!"

The portal, however, began to suck the sorcerer up into it, like an abduction. As his body was lifted off the ground, Zanabar extended his two bony arms toward the ground and tried to lower himself away from the portal. The ground shifted with the weight of his magic, although the portal's grasp was stronger.

Within seconds, Zanabar was swallowed up into the portal, which blinked out of existence soon afterward.

In the aftermath, a deafening silence followed. Frankie looked to Levi, then Evelyn, and finally to Tommy's body on the ground.

Softly, Levi broke the silence. "What did you do?"

Frankie swallowed down the remorse that had been creeping up in him over having lost Tommy, despite almost saving him. "The spell transferred Zanabar to an alternate plane. One where even he can't escape from."

"But how did you manage it when your powers were weak?" Evelyn asked. "Even at full strength, Zanabar would've been more powerful with all of the magic he had collected through the years."

"I had help from someone in my time."

"Another witch?" she asked.

Frankie shook his head, then turned to Levi. "Pure intentions are the biggest part of successful spellcasting. This person was nonmagical, like you."

"So you're saying I could cast a spell, if my intentions are true?" Levi asked.

"Only in certain circumstances," Frankie said. "And it'd have to be powered by another witch. In this case, I was powering the spell from this time while he assisting me from my time."

"Oh." Levi seemed disappointed, but let the subject drop in the aftermath of the night's events.

"Why the alternate plane?" Evelyn asked.

"After I had figured out that's where the phantoms were hiding, it gave me an idea," Frankie explained. "When I cast the spell with Hecate, that was really the test as to whether it would work or not. And I'm glad it did. Otherwise, we wouldn't have found you, Evelyn."

She mouthed a quiet, "Thank you."

"So Zanabar is trapped in the alternate plane?" Levi asked.

Frankie nodded. "Somewhere even he can't escape from."

Evelyn and Levi exchanged looks. Finally, she turned to Frankie.

"But...with Zanabar gone, then..." She trailed off and looked to Levi to finish the sentence.

"Then you can't get back home."

The thought had occurred to Frankie before. But now that everything was done—Hecate was gone; Zanabar was trapped—the weight of the realization that he would truly never return to his daughters hit Frankie with an impact that was nearly physical.

All of his remaining strength was zapped out of him. He dropped to his knees and his shoulders shook with deep sobs that emanated from his core. All he could think

Lured by Magic

about were Samantha and Kathy. They would be okay, but he would never see them again.

Never see Samantha graduate college, or Kathy graduate high school. Never see them get jobs and get married and grow into the women—and witches—that they were destined to be.

He was truly stuck in the past. And this time, there was no hope whatsoever of returning to the future.

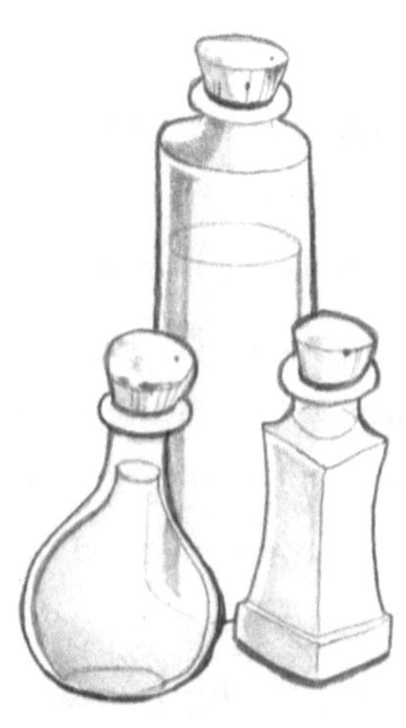

CHAPTER 47

It was interesting. Despite being sixty years in the past, funeral traditions were more or less the same. There was the solemn church service, followed by a trip to the cemetery, and rounded out with an invitation to a somber reception.

Frankie, Evelyn, and Levi sat in the front of the small chapel. It was mostly empty, only filled with coworkers from Meyer's Place. But Levi had been insistent on having a funeral service for Tommy. The young man may not have had any family left in his life by the time he had died, but Levi felt responsible for filling that void. Especially after knowing how little Tommy truly had; all of which had gone unnoticed.

Lured by Magic

After the service at Erie Cemetery, the small congregation slowly dispersed to head back to the restaurant, which had been closed for the day in Tommy's honor. Frankie, Evelyn, and Levi lagged behind as they walked through the cemetery toward the exit.

"Are you okay?" Evelyn asked Frankie. "You've been kind of quiet the last several days."

Frankie shrugged. "No, I'm not okay. And I don't know if I'm ever going to be."

She frowned. "Don't think like that. We'll find a way to—"

"Please don't," he cut in. "Don't lie. There is no other way to get me home. It's been almost two months since I've been in 1924. If there was another way to get me home, we would've found it by now. Besides, after two months in the past, there's no telling what kind of ripple effects my being here has caused. Is the future even the future that I remember? What would I really be going back to if we could even get me there?" He shook his head. "It's impossible."

Evelyn rubbed his back and rested her head on his shoulder as they walked.

"So what can we do to help?" Levi asked. "I hate seeing you like this."

Frankie thought about it as they continued to walk at

a slow pace. "I appreciate you guys trying to cheer me up. I do. But I think the best thing you can do for me is to not lie to me. Don't give me false hope." He looked down at his feet as they walked along the pavement and through the fallen leaves. "I'm never going to be okay with the fact that I can't see my daughters again. But this is the reality that I'm living in now."

"So where do we go from here?" Levi asked.

"What do you mean?" Evelyn asked.

"Do we just go on living our lives? Or do we track down every mage, wizard, or warlock out there to find a way to send you back?"

"Warlock?" Evelyn asked with a grin.

"Hey, I took a shot. I'm not sure what to believe, or not to believe, anymore."

Frankie sighed. "I don't know where we go from here. All I know is that it looks like from here on out, 1924 is my home."

Evelyn rubbed his back as they walked, but otherwise they were all quiet.

Frankie pictured Samantha and Kathy's faces. He thought about the times they had made him laugh, the things they had done that he felt so immensely proud of, and even the little things that he would miss. Coming home every day and hearing how their days went. Sitting down for dinner each night and laughing and talking —

LURED BY MAGIC

or even bickering—about any absurd topic that was on the table that night.

He thought about his magic and how, no matter how much power he had, and how many resources he had to make his power stronger, he would very likely never possess the power to ever see them again.

His only hope was that maybe someday they would come looking for him. Eventually, maybe they would be strong enough to find him, no matter where he was in the timeline. Someday, maybe he could be reunited with them.

Someday. Maybe.

BEHIND THE BOOK: LURED BY MAGIC

Unlike with *Lost by Magic* and *Lucky by Magic*, this book was the first book I wrote completely during my free periods at work. By time I finished the first draft of *Lucky by Magic*, it was right before I went back to work full time, and left me no time to start writing *Lured by Magic*. So, with no other choice, I did what I could in the forty minutes I had each day (minus the days I had classes scheduled to come in during my free periods).

As a result, this book took me longer to write the first draft than the other two. I think I started it in September 2022, and didn't finish until about halfway through November 2022. But it was done, and finishing it let a huge weight off of my shoulders.

Originally, the third book in the Lost by Magic series was going to tell the legend of the Woman in White, but I couldn't find a good enough way to tie it in with the way I needed to wrap up the Zanabar three-book story arc. So I shifted gears and used another idea I had had: Hecate.

Throughout the series I had made a point to show how even though Frankie was a powerful witch, he is still from a generation of magic where time travel isn't so commonplace. That leads him to be at the mercy of Hecate and Zanabar to get back home to his daughters, which puts him at a moral crossroads, where he has to decide to return to his daughters, or be a good witch and do what he needs to in order to make sure that evil does not run amuck in the past.

Another thing I was excited to tell was the idea of Frankie communicating with someone from 1984 through notes left behind. A long time ago I had watched a movie that involved time travel, where the character had gone back in time (maybe only a week or so) and left notes for himself to find in the future and, based on those notes, he changed the future with the small acts he made in the past. I wish I could remember what movie it was, but it was something like he cut himself in the past, only to show his future self that he was who he said he was and, as the future self read the note, he saw a scar form on his arm.

Anyway, it was a cool concept and one that I wanted to implement in this book, but I also wanted to show Eddie struggling with the note that he found from Frankie and trying to determine if he should help his friend and wrapping his head about the fact that Frankie was into some occult stuff. Again, this being 1984 when the "future" part of this book takes place, and the fear of cults and satanism was running rampant throughout the country.

Originally, I wanted to have Frankie communicate with Eddie throughout the book, much like the movie I (barely) remembered, but it didn't quite fit in with the story, so I scrapped that idea.

One of the things I did like doing with Eddie's storyline, though, was showing yet another person talking to Samantha and Kathy and asking about Frankie's whereabouts. Through that, we get to see how Samantha and Kathy handled their father's disappearance from afar. It's a nice contradiction to the Coven series, where the two of them are the main characters.

If only Samantha and Kathy had paid more attention or dug into the questions being asked about their father, maybe they could've found a way to bring him back to

Lured by Magic

their time and restored what they had missed. Of course, as we learn in the Coven series, the girls are struggling to hold their own as instant-adults, with Samantha working all the time to keep the house, all while going to college, and Kathy trying to finish her senior year of high school, while also working to pay the bills. Things teenagers shouldn't ever have to face, but that was their reality.

I hope you enjoyed reading this book as much I did writing it! If you did, please leave a review online to let other readers know what you thought of it! Every review helps add social credit to my books, so even a simply star rating or on-line review helps!

Thanks for reading!

Acknowledgments

This project would not have been possible without the support of my Kickstarter backers! Thank you all for your support!

Julian White - Pauline Baird Jones - Leslie Twitchell - John Idlor - Dead Fishie - Rhys Everly-Lawless - Debbie Phillips - Samantha Ghormley - Andrew French - Ian the Badlyironed - Karen Tankersley - Claudia Klein - Becky Carr - René Fuentes - Amber Beck - Anthea Sharp - Rowan Stone - Rachelle Degoumois - Ashley Britt - RJ Hopkinson - Hope Terrell - Chad Bowden - Daniel Dickerson - Bill Garrett - Erik S - Gary Phillips - Felicitas Odemer - Philip J. Carpenter - A

Saving him is their job, but it won't get his victim justice.

Samantha and Kathy are witches who protect the nonmagical from evil. So when they spot a coven of harpies targeting Mark, a nonmagical man, they immediately rush to save him.

With the threat of the harpies still looming over Mark, the sisters learn more about him and the target on his back. Namely, that the harpies are hunting him to drag him to hell to pay for his crimes against a young woman. However, that presents a dilemma for Samantha and Kathy: do they follow their duties as witches and save the man who harmed a young woman or do they step aside and let the harpies drag him to hell to pay for those crimes?

The clock is ticking and the longer it takes Samantha and Kathy to decide what to do, the more innocent people that will be hurt by the harpies while they wait to sink their claws into Mark.

Harpy is the first book in the Coven series, which serves as a prequel series to the Under the Moon series.

HARPY

COVEN: BOOK 1

Read on for an excerpt of the first book in
the Coven series!

DAVID NETH

CHAPTER 1

- June 1988 -

What are you going to do today?" Samantha smoothed out the hair on the sides of her head and inspected herself in the mirror. The room was a haze of hairspray and perfume.

"Running a few errands," Kathy replied from her spot at the end of her sister's bed.

"Applying to jobs?" Samantha pumped lotion into her hands and rubbed them together.

"Yes, I've got a list. I'm also going to run and get some more milk and bread, since we're out."

"Good," Samantha said. "There should be enough in the account to cover it."

"I actually have cash."

"From where?"

"I found it in my dresser," Kathy said. "Apparently I had an emergency stash I forgot about."

Samantha studied her as she finished rubbing in the lotion. She didn't like the idea of Kathy using her life savings on last-minute groceries, but they didn't really have a choice. They were short on cash. Hence, the job interview she was about to go to. Rather, the *second* job interview. The first one earlier in the week went swimmingly, which only made her nerves for the second one worse.

"You could finish those dishes in the sink, too." Samantha grabbed a comb and a mini bottle of hair spray from her dresser and stepped out of the room to descend the stairs.

"That's on my list too." Kathy followed behind. "Are you sure you want me to get a job? How else would we get all this housework done?"

Samantha stopped in her path to her purse and shot her sister a look. "We'd manage."

Collecting the copies of her résumé and the other important papers she needed for her meeting, Samantha stuffed them in an envelope and hooked them under her arm as she threw her comb and hairspray into her purse.

She had another interview with Darius Wilcox,

CPA, an accounting firm downtown. One of her former professors recommended the firm to her just before she graduated with her degree in accounting last month. It was the perfect fit and something she and Kathy desperately needed.

Samantha snatched up her keys, slung her purse over her shoulder and turned to her sister. "How do I look?"

"Very professional." Kathy beamed. "You're going to knock 'em dead! Again."

"I don't look like a wannabe college graduate?"

"No offense, but you *are* a college graduate," Kathy said. "And until someone gives you an opportunity to actually do something with it, you'll always be a wannabe."

Samantha rolled her eyes. "That's not encouraging."

"You look great, Sam. They already love you, which is why they called you back for another interview."

"Thanks."

"But, rest assured, it's certainly clear that you're the *older* sister."

Samantha rolled her eyes and pushed at Kathy's shoulder. "Yeah, and you wouldn't think one year would make that big of a difference, but here we are."

"Hey!" Kathy laughed. "What does that mean?"

HARPY

"I don't have time for this. I'm going to be late."

"You have plenty of time. Good luck and knock 'em dead!"

"Let's hope it doesn't come to that," Samantha said with a smirk.

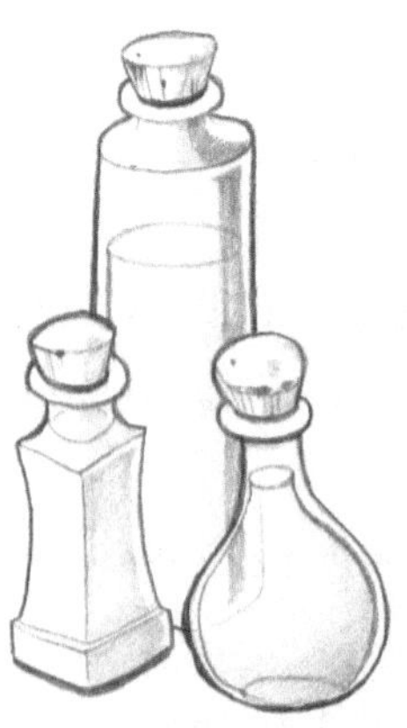

CHAPTER 2

Well, Miss Walker, you certainly have a lot to offer." Mr. Marsden offered a genuine smile and indicated Samantha's résumé and the notes he made through the interview. They were sitting at the end of the long conference table in one of the board rooms in the office suite. "Believe me, I don't tell everyone this, but you're one of our strongest candidates."

Samantha smiled. "Thank you. I've done my best to get as much experience as possible."

"I can see that." He fixed his tie and smoothed it down against his belly. "For the sake of clarity, I just like to explain the process. Typically when we take on new hires, we have them go through three rounds of interviews. We're pretty much done with the second round here. The third round—which you'll be moving on to—will consist of myself and a few other people from the firm as sort of a panel interview. From there, we'll give you a call with our decision, no matter what we choose. In all honesty, I still need to figure out who exactly is going to be on this panel, so there's some details on our side that still need to be worked out."

She nodded. "Okay. That sounds fair. Thank you for seeing me again today."

"Absolutely, thanks for coming down." He stood and came around the table and extended his hand. "It was nice to see you again. Take care and we'll be in touch."

Samantha shook his hand and thanked him again before exiting the office.

Down in the lobby, she dug some spare change from the bottom of her purse and fed it into a free payphone, among the long line of them. When she heard the dial tone, she dialed the house and waited for her sister to pick up, hoping Kathy was back already from her errands.

Samantha needed to tell someone the good news right away and her boyfriend Steven was at work at a different accounting firm. Kathy was the only one she knew would be free.

"Hello?" Kathy answered on the last ring.

"It's me."

"Oh! How'd it go? Did you get the job?"

"Not yet, but it's looking that way," she said. "He told me I'm moving on to the next round."

"The next round?"

"Yeah, the next round of interviews."

"Geez, how many rounds are there?" Kathy asked. "It feels like you've been interviewing there forever."

"It's been two interviews."

"Well, is this next one the last one?"

"Should be." Samantha swatted at the air. The man two payphones down was smoking. She wished they would make it illegal to smoke indoors. She hated breathing it in. "Anyway, I called because I thought we should celebrate. Do you want to go to lunch?"

"Sure! But aren't we tight on money?"

"I'm about to have a new job."

Kathy laughed. Samantha was usually the one who didn't count on anything until it was a sure thing, so the fact that Samantha herself was predicting landing this job was a statement.

"Okay," Kathy said with a chuckle. "You heading out now?"

"Yeah, I should be there to pick you up in about fifteen minutes. Be ready."

"I'm on it, boss."

CHAPTER 3

Mark Gad tapped his pen on the updated privacy policy packet in front of him. It was marked up with notes and doodles he made during the meeting, which was still dragging on.

He looked up at the clock and saw that it was 11:57. His stomach growled, but most of all he was craving a cigarette. He finished his last one just before the meeting at his desk. The fact that several of his coworkers sitting around the conference table were puffing on their own smokes made his craving worse.

Finally, Mr. Bellman, the Senior VP of Communications at Blue Water Insurance, announced that the meeting was adjourned and every man seated around the conference table shot to his feet and rushed to the door to start their lunch break.

Mark tossed his packet on his desk in the cubicle space the higher-ups had the audacity to call his office. He grabbed his keys, wallet, and ID, and walked through the makeshift hallway around other cubicle "offices" to the lobby, where he stood amongst other workers waiting for the elevator to take them down.

When the doors opened, everyone crammed into the elevator, invading personal space and pretending like it wasn't a problem. Acting like this behavior was perfectly normal. The sad part was that it had become the lunchtime routine now that the weather broke. Everyone was desperate to get outside and enjoy the sunshine, even if only for thirty minutes a day.

Once he got out onto the sidewalk, Mark stepped into the small hole-in-the-wall convenience store in the corner storefront of his office building. It was quiet in there and he relished in the silence as he browsed the shelves for something to snack on for lunch—he forgot his leftovers at home.

Opening the refrigerator in the back of the store, Mark pulled out a box of Hot Pockets and reached for a bottle of Cherry 7UP from the top shelf. He brought his goodies to the counter and told the cashier he wanted a pack of Marlboros.

After he paid, Mark stepped out on the street, dug through the plastic bag, and retrieved his cigarettes. He opened the celofane, tapped out a smoke, and brought it to his mouth to light it.

Finally satisfied now that he had a good drag, Mark himself started to enjoy the beautiful weather they were having. Cloudless sky, people passing by on the sidewalk, cars whizzing by on the street with the windows down. Summer weather was here for the season.

With the plastic bag digging into his palm from the heavy 7UP bottle, Mark set it on the sidewalk next to the building until he finished his cigarette. He slipped the pack into his pocket and took another look up at the beautiful blue sky.

To his right, he caught of glimpse of three birds flying through the air further down State Street. As if sensing him looking, they turned and started their direction up the street, growing larger as they approached.

Mark's smoke clung to his bottom lip as he stared up at the trio in confusion, mouth hung slack. Now that they were closer and he had a good look at them, the birds looked different. Almost with a *human* face. And they looked to be about the size of a regular person. Worse, they seemed to be charging toward him.

Turning, he tossed his cigarette on the ground and

HARPY

moved toward the door to the office building, not wanting to risk stopped to pick up what he bought for lunch.

The birds swung low, swiping at Mark's arm as he grabbed the door handle to the office building. He ducked out of the way before they could attack him again, but now they were blocking his way into the building.

One of them looped through the air and looked to be winding up to take another shot, but Mark wasn't going to risk it. He broke into a run down the sidewalk with the three birds hot in pursuit.

TO READ THE REST OF **HARPY**,
ORDER YOUR COPY AT
DAVIDNETHBOOKS.COM/COVEN

FIND ALL THE BOOKS IN THE COVEN SERIES!

More by the Author

To find more books by the author, visit
DavidNethBooks.com/Books

* * *

Subscribe to his newsletter to be the first to know of new
releases and special deals!
DavidNethBooks.com/Newsletter

* * *

**If you enjoyed the book, please consider leaving a
review on Goodreads or the retailer you bought it from.**
Reviews help potential readers determine whether
they'll enjoy a book, so any comments on what you
thought of the story would be very helpful!

ABOUT THE AUTHOR

David Neth is the author of the Lost by Magic series, the Coven series, the Under the Moon series, the Heat series, the Fuse series, and other stories. He lives in Batavia, NY, where he dreams of opening his own bookstore.

Also writes small town romance as D. Allen.

www.DavidNethBooks.com

www.facebook.com/DavidNethBooks